OUR SECRET'S OUT

OUR SECRET'S OUT

Stories by
Darrell Spencer

UNIVERSITY OF MISSOURI PRESS
COLUMBIA AND LONDON

Copyright © 1993 by Darrell Spencer
University of Missouri Press, Columbia, Missouri 65201
Printed and bound in the United States of America
All rights reserved
5 4 3 2 1   97 96 95 94 93

Library of Congress Cataloging-in-Publication Data
Spencer, Darrell, 1947–
  Our secret's out : stories / by Darrell Spencer.
    p. cm.
  ISBN 0–8262–0927–0 (alk. paper)
  I. Title.
PS3569.P44609 1993
813'.54—dc20   93–4855
                                             CIP

∞ This paper meets the requirements of the American National Standard for Permanence of Paper for Printed Library Materials, Z39.48, 1984.

Designer: Elizabeth K. Fett
Typesetter: Connell-Zeko Type & Graphics
Printer and Binder: Thomson-Shore, Inc.
Typeface: Cochin

Some of the stories in this collection first appeared in the following publications: "Song and Dance" in *High Plains Literary Review*; "Halloween" in *Epoch*; "Union Business" is reprinted from *Prairie Schooner* by permission of the University of Nebraska Press, copyright 1991 University of Nebraska Press; "As Long As Lust Is Short" in *Epoch*; "Hops" in *The Quarterly*; "The Glue That Binds Us" in the *Cimarron Review* and is reprinted here with the permission of the Board of Regents for Oklahoma State University, holders of the copyright; "Let Me Tell You What Ward DiPino Tells Me at Work" in *Epoch*; "Loose in the Mail" in the Spring 1991 issue of *The Gettysburg Review* and is reprinted by permission of the editors; "Nothing Sad, Once You Look at It" in *High Plains Literary Review*; "My Home State of Nevada" in *Quarterly West*; and "Lake Stink" in *Epoch*.

The song "The Shooting of Dan McGrew" is reprinted by permission of Running Press, Philadelphia, PA, from *Robert W. Service: Best Tales of the Yukon*, by Robert W. Service, copyright 1983 by Running Press.

*For Kate, always;
and for François Camoin*

CONTENTS

Song and Dance 1

Halloween 24

Union Business 32

My Home State of Nevada 49

Nothing Sad, Once You Look at It . . 51

Lake Stink 69

Our Secret's Out 87

Loose in the Mail 104

As Long As Lust Is Short 115

Hops 127

The Glue That Binds Us 134

Let Me Tell You What Ward DiPino
Tells Me at Work 152

OUR SECRET'S OUT

Song and Dance

Boomtown Tonopah, Nevada, ended its isolation from the world on July 4, 1903, when Tosker L. Oddie banged and jolted a Ford sixty miles over the one washboard road ore-filled wagons had pounded into the desert from the railroad spur at Sodaville to the three tents and one frame house that made up the mining site. One day this Republican attorney Tosker L. Oddie would be filthy rich and governor of the Silver State.

How I end up in Tonopah eighty-five years later spending my mornings knocking lopsided golf balls into the mesquite and sagebrush south of town and my afternoons at a twenty-one table in the Mizpah Hotel, Chinese exercise balls in one hand rotating and chiming up and over each other, while my other hand flicks *hit me* and *hold*, how I wind up here begins in Las Vegas, Nevada, the day I unshoetree my Aldens and buff them crisp as beetles, then ride an elevator the nine floors to Uncle Beaner's office in the Circus Circus, where I take my best shot at Beaner, which, I'll learn later, he calls a song and dance, a floor show.

I wag my tie at Mona, Uncle Beaner's niece, his secretary.
"Flashy," she says.
I've made an appointment. It's businesslike.
"Go in," she says.
Frederick J. Bean's got this Boston lawyer's office floating above the neon of Vegas. The scene I expect is him jumping up and coming around his nine-yard-deep cherrywood desk and saying, "Jay, my boy." What I am hoping for is a clap on the

back one man to another and the repositioning of a soft chair for me. What I get is him, head down, one hand held up and flat out, saying, *Sit down. Don't talk.*

My plan is simple. He loans me two hundred thousand dollars, and I go to Hawaii where I play golf ten hours a day for one year. Then I hit the Q-School, qualify for the pro tour, and pay him back plus interest.

I've brought along what the newspapers say about me. The *Las Vegas Sun* says, "Learn how to spell this young man's name." I'd just won the Silver State Amateur. I tore up Northgate in Reno, going seven under the last day. The *Review Journal* named me Nevada's athlete of the year. I've jotted down names of pros Beaner can call. They're willing to talk. They're *happy* to talk.

I can sit over drinks with the best and b.s. about the music of the great courses, and I'm willing to put on coveralls and labor in a machine shop to grind the bounce out of my wedge. The golf swing is a series of slides in my head. Clubhead speed matters, but it's time of contact, it's the longer the ball's on the face of the club, that adds up to yards down the middle. What did particle physics do for the golf ball? Ask me. How many dimples on a Titleist? I'll tell you. Three hundred and eighty-four. I'm no flake. Long grass? The rough? I not only understand its nastiness, I applaud it. I'd vote to make it worse. I can open up the club face on a four iron, drop it onto a ball that's sat down in six inches of junk, and pop it out two hundred yards if I have to.

Once I get Uncle Beaner's attention I don't lie. I don't hold back. There was the nine iron I cold-shanked when I was fifteen. I've not let one fly since, but the feel of it's not gone, and it stinks in the palm of my hands. It's a woodpecker in my head. Even now, I stand over a nine iron, and my balls tighten up. There's a crawling like something's gotten in my shorts. My answer is I knock most nine irons in low and soft as ducks and let them run at the pin. Also, my two iron tails.

What I need is one year. That's all I'm asking for.

"Give me facts," Beaner says. The top of his head's bumpy

and more pointed than round and is stitched by tiny sprigs of black hair. The skin's vaguely blue.

I hold out the newspaper clippings. They verify I've not lost an event I've entered since the day I turned fourteen and destroyed everybody in the Western State Juniors.

He bats at them and says, "Talk to me."

I say, "I can't get a game for money from even the local pros." I point out the phone numbers of the big names I have. "Telephone," I say.

He says, "What are the odds?"

"No odds," I say. "This is not gambling. No one would cover a bet on this. I'm a shoo-in." I thumb through the articles he's tossed aside, and I again read off the names of the pros who'll talk for me. I say, "At the Qualifying School I shoot fifteen under. The next Monday you pick up the sports page and the headline says, ROOKIE WINS GREATER GREENS-BORO. I've broken Nicklaus's record. Before you can flap the page back, Federal Express is at your door having you sign an envelope that contains seventy thousand dollars, your fifty percent of what I won. Week after, same story. Monday mornings, Federal Express is a regular at your front door. You get to know the delivery people. You call them by first names. In two months I've paid you what you loaned me plus interest, and you look like a man who sees a winner when you see one."

I talk, and his muscley pent-up arms ride his desk. His watch is closer to his elbow than to his wrist. He's about to fry me.

"Your own brother," I say, "my father, took no lessons and qualified for The Open, where he posted a seventy-one and a seventy-three before he got a wild hair up his ass and loop in his swing."

"Rule number one," Beaner says, and he gets up. Behind him are photos of him and Yogi Berra, of him and Frank Sinatra, of him and Siegfried and Roy, the lion tamers. There's a king of the beasts on its back in front of them. Beaner says, "No such thing as a shoo-in." He's coming around the desk. He's a rhino, a galoot.

I say, "On a bet, I shot eighty blindfolded. I broke my ankle and turned in a sixty-seven at the Dunes."

He covers his mouth, then tugs at his chin. He's in his stocking feet and is wiggling his toes.

I untuck my shirt, pull it up, and whack myself in the stomach. "Brick hard," I say. I tell him how much I run and show him my calves.

He says, "Why two hundred thousand?"

I've checked out the cost of Hawaii. I did my homework. Like the businessman I am, I lay it out for Beaner.

"Why Hawaii?" he says.

I say, "Arizona? Maybe Southern Cal, San Diego."

Uncle Beaner's taken my arm and is helping me up. I'm a foot taller and thirty years younger and I'm aware he could put me through a wall.

He says, "Nice tie," and flips it. "And shoes."

My crisp shoes embarrass me.

"I'll see," he says. "My decision will come from here." He lays a finger across his heart. "Not from here." He pokes his head. The sideways look he gives me is the one you save for the lunatic on the bus who's obviously lost touch with how things are.

He's got me outside his office and is gone before I can say, "I could win at Augusta. I can smell the honeysuckle." Mona sends me a baby's cute little bye-bye wave and says, "Come back soon."

What I can't do is hide the fact that I'm a college dropout who somehow ran through the twenty thousand dollars his father gives his kids when they graduate from high school. The idea is we can do what we want, but it's clear he's rooting for college. I went to UNLV and almost made two years, then sold my textbooks for half of cost and fled. So when my dad asks me to come by his office I know Beaner's called him.

My father doesn't say, *Jay, my boy. Come in. Please, sit. Coffee?* No. What he says is, "Uncle Beaner tells me you're doing some song and dance about Hawaii and the pro tour and forty percent of two hundred thousand dollars."

I tell him it's a business proposition.

"It's a floor show," he says. He tells me Beaner's gotten me a job at Juvenile Hall.

"Nice of him," I say.

"He pulled strings," my father says. "You're not really old enough."

I say, "Wonderful."

"You've got other possibilities?" he says. "You have irons in some red hot fire? Adventures up your sleeves? Better more convincing songs to sing?"

I'm not twenty-one, and I am a flunk-out, a runner from the important stuff. Besides, I'm broke. I say, "When do I start?"

He says, "You train tomorrow, and you work nights." He folds up a check he's already written out and slips it into my shirt pocket. He says, "Find an apartment."

The check's message is it's the last leaf of the money tree.

The job at JuVee is in booking, and Julio Guia is the guy who trains me. Good boy that I am, I come in early. Julio looks me over like he's going to buy me. He's wearing a beret that has rows of buttons pinned along one side. Mostly they're of rock singers. One's of Stalin. Julio's got a greedy face, and he's wearing a yellow singlet. He says, "A new man, huh?"

We start on a computer. "It walks you through it," Julio says to me. The desk we're behind is one you'd see in a library where they check books out. We're high up.

Julio gives me a name, and I tap it in. The computer says, "Par:d/n."

"That kid comes in," Julio says, "and you call his parole officer *day* or *night*." He points to the d and the n, then shows me how to access the parole officer's name and phone number. He says, "No one gets that info. No one. For no reason. No matter what they say. If they say, 'He's my son. I'm dying,' you say, 'This is sad. Hope it's not painful. I'll reach him for you.' You get a number, and you call the parole officer with it."

I feed names into the computer, and Julio reads a paperback he has. I'm being led through practice bookings. There's a lot of *what if this happens?* and *what if that happens?*

Julio finishes a page of his book and tears it out. Pages are stacked loosely on the counter.

I get us Cokes.

Julio says to me, "You read?"

I say, "I can."

"You read this," he says, "and it'll make you angry." He rips out a page. The book's *Johnny Got His Gun*. He says, "It's about war."

I tell him I'll read it.

"It's yours," he says. "When I'm done." He shuffles the pages together and puts a rubberband around them. They hump up.

Two highway patrolmen buzz the outside door, and Julio pushes the button that unlocks it. To me he says, "Always look." From where we sit, we can see who's at the door through the thick glass windows on each side of it. Julio says, "If they're not where you can see them, tell everyone to stand where you can." He shows me how to work the intercom. The highway patrolmen bring in a boy who's handcuffed. The kid could do TV ads. He's got cherry red lips, and his hair sweeps across his forehead like a sand dune.

"Hey," Julio says to the cops.

They rattle around and pull at their clothes. They can't settle in one spot. One pats his shoulder. They get up on their toes, rock back and forth, and their shoes squeak. It's like they're doing a cop skit. One says, "Kid's a transfer."

"All yours," Julio says to me.

I say, "Name?" I'm looking down on the boy.

His voice is a girl's, and he's not old enough to have a chin yet. I run a record check. None. I get his age, which is eleven. I type in his address, his school, and ask for his parents' names, mother first.

"Irene," he says.

I feed it in and say, "Father?"

He says, "Dead."

I move the cursor over and type *deceased*, then take it back and say, "What was his name?"

The boy says, "Adam."

I type it.

He says, "He's not my real father. My last name's not his." I put down *stepfather*.

One of the highway patrolmen says, "Smith. Adam Smith. We don't think he married the mother."

I say to him, "Charge?"

He says, "Murder."

There is something in his voice. He's not angry. That's not it. He doesn't care. This is duty. Maybe what it is is malice. Maybe it's boredom. Or stupidity. Whatever it is he's set it loose, and it's gone to the corner of the room where it begins to grow.

When I finish the booking sheet, I phone detention and escort the boy over to the door. One of the highway patrolmen comes with us. Julio is talking to the other one. The supervisor from detention opens up, and he and the cop say hello. They seem to be buddies. Behind us, Julio and the other cop slap hands. The one who is with me unlocks the handcuffs, then swings them around, and drops them in a pouch on his belt.

I let the highway patrolmen out the front door. You have to do that. You unlock the door, then shut it after they've gone. You have to push on the door until you hear its lock click.

I say to Julio, "What was that?"

He taps his cheek with his book.

"With the cop," I say.

"His thanks and my gratitude," Julio says. "I'm giving him facts for Rodriguez."

"Like a movie," I say.

"Info," he says. "Facts. I sell facts."

I say, "Facts?"

"You get to know what's going on, and you make money."

"A snitch?"

"An informant," he says.

"What?" I say. "Drugs. Buying and selling?"

"Jesus," he says. "I sell info, facts. I'm an informant." He turns around and says, "See? Eyes in the back of my head. I give dates and names. And Rodriguez, he buys." Julio spins on his stool and lifts out his legs. His pants are peach, and they're pin-striped. He says, "Check it out." He stands up. The pants are pleated and flappy as a flag. He holds them away from his legs. They fit tight around his ankles. He says, "The feet. One-hundred-dollar running shoes. Rodriguez looks good. I look good. You know, do unto others." The shoes are a little like house slippers. They glitter.

I say, "Nice."

"Facts," he says.

Later, when I ask, Julio tells me the kid I booked in shot his stepfather. The mother coaxed him into it. She said, "Honey, listen to me. He hurts me." She showed the boy. She unbuttoned her blouse, hiked up her skirt. There were cuts and bruises. She loaded the rifle—a 30.06, Julio says—and talked to the guy so the kid could sneak up behind him. After the boy shot the stepfather, the mother went out and got some fried chicken, and she and the boy were sitting at the kitchen table, the dead man under their feet, his head in a towel, when a neighbor looked in, saw the body, and called the police.

Training lasts four hours, then I go to the Desert Inn's driving range. I hit nothing but two irons. I'm buck-and-winging it. I'm hot. My body's sizzling. It's singing, *Turn the shoulders against the hips. Rocket the right side through.* For an hour I don't miss sweet dead center. I tug a bucket of balls ten feet six inches left of my target, then push another bucket ten feet six inches to the right. I lace half a dozen right at it. Then one tails. Golf is more mind than body. I run pictures of my swing through my head. Problem is I'm wagging the clubhead at the top. I think, Ball-striking is brain not body, and I adjust the film. In my mind the clubhead's steady. But the next shot tails. I strap three more right at the target, then grieve when they fall off. They miss the path I've set for them like bad dogs.

I pack up and head for the apartment I found. It's quiet and can be made dark as night during the day. It's what I'll need to sleep. The check my father gave me was for five thousand dollars.

My first night shift at JuVee is mostly kids who are out after curfew. Only the ones who bad-mouth the cops end up here. The others get citations. Then they keep doing what they're doing. I book the ones the cops bring in and call their parents.

Julio's left me *Johnny Got His Gun*, the pages held together by a rubberband. Inside the cover, he's written, *This will piss you off.* It's full of hippie thoughts, of shit the world would rather forget. I don't want to hear it. About three, the outside door buzzes, and I see two Metro cops. They've got a girl with them who looks twenty-five. She's melt-your-socks gorgeous. Her clothes are military, Civil War–looking, all brass buttoned and gold embroidered. She's got on leggings and heavy let-me-stomp-on-you boots. Around her neck is a black leather choker crisscrossed in the front. It's got spikes on it. Her hair is orange and all frizzed up.

I ask her name, and she says, "Ta-mar-a."

Her file comes up. She's fifteen. I punch keys, and the computer fills in most of the booking sheet. I say, "Tonight's charge."

She says, "Trolling."

One of the cops says, "Soliciting."

I type it in.

"Trick and treating," she says.

I finish up and phone detention. A woman comes out and stands with her back against the door to keep it from shutting. Someone yells inside. The woman's head is turned away from me. Someone calls someone else a butt-face. I walk Tamara over, and the woman says, "Thank you. We've got a kid gone more than a little crazy in here." Glass breaks down the hallway.

The woman takes Tamara's arm and says to me, "I'm Alison." Her eyes are green, and her face is Snow White's. She's reaching across her body to shake my hand.

I say, "Jay."

I let the cops out and lock up behind them, and I'm reading a magazine when Alison comes in. She says, "Drink?" and unscrews the cap from a bottle of Bacardi.

"Here?" I say.

She fills a cup for herself. Her forearm is ringed from her wrist to her elbow with silver bracelets that slide together and clang when she drinks.

She says, "I'm the boss." Her hair jumps straight up from one spot near the top of her head and then falls in shingles. It's black, so black it's a deep purple in streaks. Above each eye is a fan of green.

"This is a test, isn't it?" I say. "It's like being a cop on duty, and you're giving a pop quiz to the new kid in town."

She pours rum into a second cup, hands it to me, and says, "To the new kid in town."

We touch cups.

I drink, then I say, "That girl?"

Alison says, "You can't afford her."

"How much?" I say.

"Call her service. You've got her number." She points at the booking sheet I've printed up. She says, "You old enough to drink?"

I say, "Soon."

We drink Bacardi and talk until two highway patrolmen drag in a black kid who is doing a nightclub routine from the time I open the door until I get him booked in. He's dressed for the stage. He's got on tuxedo pants and tap shoes. He sees Alison and says, "Hey, Al."

She says, "Hey, Breeze."

The only name he'll give me is Cool Breeze. I plug it in and cross-reference for aliases. His name is Stanford Tucker. Everybody knows him. I call his parole officer, and he tells me to hold him for a hearing. At the door to detention, Cool Breeze raises his hands as if to say *no tricks up my sleeve.* He rolls his eyes, then claps my shoulders. He reaches out and leads me through some kind of double-jointed screwy handshake, and I'm left holding a joint. It's like he's tipped me.

Alison takes off. I pick through some pages of *Johnny Got His Gun* but can't finish even one paragraph. It's more talk than action, and Julio's not put the pages in order.

At five, Alison brings me a small box of cereal, Froot

Song and Dance

Loops, and a carton of milk. She pulls up a stool. She brought Frosted Flakes for herself.

She is sitting beside me, and I say, "Just like fifth grade."

"Not something I do for just anyone," she says.

We light Cool Breeze's joint. She goes first, then I take it. It sickens the Froot Loops I've eaten. She opens her Bacardi.

I say, "Cool Breeze, what's his story?"

"Everyone knows Cool Breeze," she says and hands me the rum. She dumps her cereal and mine in a trash can.

I say, "He's a thief."

"A lot," she says.

I say, "Are you really the boss?"

"At night, I am. I have a Ph.D.," she says. "I'm twenty-eight, and I have a little girl. I could be your mother. Right now, this is what I do."

I say, "Golf is what I do."

"Little white balls and clubs?"

"I'm good."

She says, "What does that make you?"

"I could be a pro," I say.

She says, "How old?"

"Soon to be twenty-one," I say.

She wets her fingers, sizzles out the joint, and puts it in her pocket. She waves her arms in the air. She says, "Time to grow up?"

I'm drinking her rum.

She says, "Will you come to dinner?"

"Tonight?"

"Sometime. To my place?"

"Of course."

"Me and my little girl. She's seven."

I tell her I have sisters. I rag out the mouth of the rum and give it to her.

She drinks, then says, "This is shit work. I go to college, and I didn't do it to do this." She's picked up some pages of *Johnny Got His Gun*. She reads Julio's note, *This will piss you off.* She says, "What doesn't piss us off?"

I say, "It's about war."
"You read?" she says.
I tell her I went to college.
She says, "Not everyone reads."
I say, "You're hogging the rum."
She gets up and slaps the bottle into my hand, "Take it out of here when you go." She's wearing blue jeans and saggy brown boots. Her bracelets collect at her wrists. Halfway through the door to detention, she turns around and says to me, "Only in your dreams."

It's light outside when I get off, but the sun isn't up over Sunrise Mountain yet. In the parking lot, Bobbi, a woman who works with Alison, is standing by her car. She's holding a flower.
I stop and say, "Great day."
She says to me, "Third time this week."
I say, "The flower?"
"On the seat. On my side, where I drive. Three times now."
Alison has come out and she says, "Another lily?"
Bobbi nods.
"Your husband?" I say.
"Not my husband," she says. "I tell him and all he gets is mad."
Alison says, "Be careful," and walks on by.
I back out and come up behind Alison. At the stop sign before pulling onto Bonanza, I spot Bobbi in my rearview mirror. She hasn't gotten into her car. She's in a bright pink suit, and she is holding the lily. I slip into the traffic, then look over. She smells the lily, then, her face lifted toward the sun, she turns completely around one time.

For three weeks, I do my job at JuVee and play golf when I get off. My game's solid. I sleep when I can, which isn't often. Sleep is hard in the daytime. It comes, but it's full of noise.
Cool Breeze is brought in two or three times a week. Once he is barefoot and wearing a straw cowboy hat big enough for

the thirty-foot Vegas Vic down on Fremont Street. Sometimes Breeze is cut up. His eyes might be swollen. You can see that how he acts has irked the cop. Still, Breeze always has a story to tell. He acts like he's got a mike and says, *You got to hear this. So, I'm at the Food Mart and* . . . The thing about Cool Breeze is that being in a room with him is like being part of a juggling act. He's tossing you bowling pins faster and faster, and you've got to keep up.

If I don't book him, he calls.

Like tonight, I answer and I hear, "This the great white golfer?" He offers me any set of clubs I want for twenty-percent off what I'd pay at a pro shop. He guarantees two-week delivery. And golf balls? I name my brand. Titleist? Of course. Pro Trajectory or Pinnacle? He's got in stock and for cost whatever ball I play.

I say, "Breeze."

He says, "Listen."

I can tell he's holding the phone out. I don't hear anything.

"Can you believe it?" he says.

"What?" I say.

He says, "Hear it? Listen."

I do, but can't hear what he wants me to.

"Snoring like a bear," Cool Breeze says. "Like a fat smelly bear."

I say, "What are you doing?"

"I'm in this white man's house."

I say, "Breeze."

He says, "Can you hear how this man sleeps?"

I say, "Breeze, get out of there."

"I'm petting his Doberman," he says. "I'm loving up the dog's ears."

I say, "Don't tell me."

"This is not a problem," he says. "I'm in, I'm out. The snoring white bear don't miss what he don't miss."

Breeze always has something for me when I book him. He's given me a fourteen-karat gold tee and a trick ball marker. His plan is to be rich before he's certified as an adult. From eighteen on, he's clean. He's a whistle, he says. They toss his record. They'll expunge him. "I'll be clean, waxed, polished, pure," he says. "Not a mark on my adult record. I'll marry and produce kids, and they'll be your kids' doctors."

The outside buzzer cuts us off. I say, "Breeze, get out of there."

"The only way," he says.

I check the window and see what looks like a busload of cops and kids. It takes me two hours to book them. There's been a fight, and most of the kids have possession added on. They all have parole officers.

I don't see Alison all night, but we walk out together when our shift's over. We stop at the back of her car. She says, "Dinner next week?"

"That's good," I say.

We're facing the corner of the parking lot where Bobbi's husband is sitting in a truck. The truck's black and wrapped up in a lot of chrome. He's been out here for a week now, and there have been no lilies. He's huge, fills up the cab of his truck. Bobbi had him come in and talk to all of us so we'd know him and not call the cops.

"Next week for sure," Alison says.

I say, "Count me in. I'll bring the rum."

I get breakfast at the DI and hook up with Beaner and my father for eighteen holes. They ask for three shots a side, and I still take them for five hundred dollars. Beaner can score, but he swings like a giraffe walks. Every time he steps out of his cart, he sticks on an ugly sawed-off straw hat. He wears black socks and Hawaiian-print shorts. His legs are white as paper. For his eyes only, I strap a two iron across the lake at eighteen. It comes in screaming, then lifts like it's hit a pillow of air and drops pin-high five feet to the right of the cup. You'd think I had something going with the devil. I swagger up to the ball and backhand my putt home.

We eat lunch, and Beaner says, "The five hundred you took

us for plus another five hundred says your old man can beat you left-handed. One hole, and he'll use only his putter."

"I pick the hole," I say.

My dad agrees.

I choose a par five.

Dad says, "I'll add five hundred to Bean's."

Okay, I'm not stupid. I know. Don't play another man's game. But I can't pass on this one. I take my father's hand, then Beaner's. While he's got me, Beaner says, "A tie's his," and he nods at my father.

I say, "A tie's his. Fair's fair."

The par five is an easy reach in two, but my two iron approach tails, and the shot drifts into stiff rough. My dad's down the middle a hundred and twenty-five yards a shot, and he's left himself in a front bunker in four. He's got his trouble. I've got mine.

He says, "Let's freshen the bet. Another five hundred, and I get to use a wedge from here."

Suppose he flips the sand shot in and shoots five. I still get down in two and walk away with fifteen hundred. We shake on the bet.

I'm away, and I flop my wedge in tight, but it doesn't hold. It kicks then rolls twenty feet past. My dad pops his out, and the ball finds the hole like it's on a string. He's home in five. My four lips the edge of the cup. The tie's his. I walk up and slam the ball into the water hazard.

Thanks is what they say to my checks.

I go home and don't sleep. Two months' rent is gone. An hour before I leave for JuVee, my dad phones. He's too big a man to gloat. "Nice game," he says. "You can play."

"No shit," I say.

He says, "Does that make you something? I've stood by the best. The ball they hit is different. They have something you don't."

I say, "I know. I'm good, and I'm also not stupid."

He says, "Beaner tells me JuVee pays well. The parole

officers, the directors—they make decent money and benefits help."

I tell him I'm looking forward to moving up the ranks.

He says, "Anyone can be a smart ass."

I agree.

Two days later I'm nine hundred dollars up on a club member when he presses me on eighteen and my two iron tails. I'm left with a chip I shank. It squirts into a bunker and leaves a smooth trail. You'd think a snake had gotten into the sand.

When Alison says *golf* it comes out like an egg she's swallowed as part of a trick. She says, "Do you wear checked pants and sweaters that button over your belly?"

I reach for her Bacardi.

She unscrews the lid, drinks, then passes me the bottle. Tonight's jewelry is plastic, seven hoops up one forearm and one on the opposite bicep, plus a hoop on her left ear. Her hair curls along her cheeks.

I wipe out the mouth of the bottle.

She says, "Shoes with flaps over the top?"

I drink her rum.

"Are you twenty-one yet?" she says.

I say, "Soon."

Right now, we both know one thing. I'm not good enough to be a pro. If I was, would I be sitting here drinking rum?

She says, "The sky's the limit."

I hand her her bottle.

She says, "This is shit work."

One night, we went into one of the offices and got after each other. She works out, and I could see it. I do love women's bodies. Her muscles talked about themselves, and there was that line down the center of her stomach. We were half into it when the outside buzzer cut us off. I had to book three black girls. They were all about four feet tall. Two detectives picked them up running down the street carrying shotguns. Alison took them to detention and didn't come back out. For three days, she stayed away. Bobbi came out to get the girls I booked in.

The result is now Alison and I only talk. If I touch her, she says, "I could be your mother."

Tonight I say, "I ought to stop drinking before I'm old enough to begin."

"Probably," she says.

I go to parties and wake up in rooms I didn't enter. Music is on and maybe a TV with no sound. All day people tell me what I did, and they say, "God, were you out of it." One night, I'm lying on a floor, carpet under me, my eyes wide open, and I'm talking to some guy, but I can't see him. He's asking questions, and I'm answering. I know him from when we went to high school. I make sense, I think. But I'm blind. I don't mean it's like the light's off or it's night. My eyes are open and it's black. There is his voice, and no body, no head, no form. His voice is saying things, and I'm saying things.

I tell Alison all this, and she says, "Don't drink. You can't."

I reach for the Bacardi and say, "One last swig. The last taste of my rummy life."

She watches me, then shuts her eyes.

I say, "Save me," and hand her the bottle.

"Being mother to one child is enough for me," she says.

She dials Bobbi's house because Bobbi didn't come in. I called earlier, and we're not getting an answer. Alison says, "Try in half an hour, will you?" Then she heads for detention.

I never reach Bobbi. In the morning, on the way home, I stop at the DI and hit nine irons. They rise and fall and fill the air like sprinkler water. It's the weekend.

When I get back to work I hear Bobbi is dead. For a week we listen to stories. TVs are on at work, people hoping for any news. They say it's murder. Everyone at JuVee has a detail to add. She was run off the road and strangled. They found flesh under her fingernails. She was raped. There was a lily on her lap.

Her husband's interviewed on the late news. He offers a reward and he cries. He shakes like a building.

Alison says, "This ain't worth it."

"You worried?" I say.

She says, "Name a place where people don't kill people."

"Idaho," I say. "It's too cold. They only kill animals. They use bows and arrows, something you could dodge."

She says, "Nazis."

"Nazis."

"In Idaho," she says. "You told me you read. Idaho's full of Nazis. Read a newspaper once a year. The hills of Idaho are full of skinheads and Nazis. And dead cows in the fields. Nuts cut them up because god has told them to."

"Montana," I say.

She says, "God, do you even watch TV, the news? They found some religion smuggling in machine guns, tanks, jets. Building bomb shelters big as cities."

I shrug and drink her rum.

She says, "Golf. You come here. You drink my rum. You go play golf, and then you come back here."

I say, "Mommy."

She says, "I'm packing up, and my little girl and me, we're going."

I say, "Utah."

"Utah," she says.

I say, "Me, too," and I offer her the Bacardi. "But not Utah. My golf game's shit. I'm stinking up the courses. I can't find the hole, and the sixteen-year-olds are beating me."

She says, "And you're getting a belly."

I say, "Tonopah."

She says, "Up the road?"

I say, "Up the road. They're building a golf course to get tourists. They'll need a pro, and no one who can play worth crap is going to want to be a pro in Tonopah, Nevada. I'll take along my clippings and show them what I've got. Think they've heard of me?"

In the morning I let Alison out, and I'm typing up a booking sheet when the door buzzes. It's her. She's come right back, and she is banging on the door. She comes in yelling.

"Jesus," she says. "No no no. I can't. Shit. Shit. Shit." She's holding a lily.

"Your car?" I say.

"On the seat, where I drive."

I pick up the phone to call the police.

"I quit," she says. "Now. This minute. Not one more minute."

She rings the boys' side of detention, and when the supervisor comes out she throws her keys at him. She says, "I'm gone. You don't know me. Tell them I'll call about how to get my check."

On the phone, I'm explaining what's happened to some cop, and I show the supervisor the lily.

He says, "Alison."

She says, "No." To me she says, "Open the door."

I point at the phone.

She screams. She says, "Out. The door. Shit."

I buzz it open, then get off the phone. I catch her at her car. We're both looking around like we're in the bad part of a big city. She gets in and locks her doors. She opens the window and says, "Here." She's gotten into her glove box and is giving me two hollow chrome balls. She rotates them in her hand, and they chime. The sound is beyond anything I've ever heard. It's the desert at night. It's concrete proof of life on other plants. She says, "Try it."

I do, and they sing for me.

"The Chinese," she says. "Calm." She asks me to lean in, and she kisses me, quick, light. She's a moth on my lips. She says, "We should have finished what we started."

All I can say is, "Yes."

She says, "I'm unglued here."

I can see she is. Over in the corner is the place where Bobbi's husband parked night after night. I say, "We never had dinner."

"Maybe we will," she says. She pulls hair on my arm. She says, "Don't let them think I'm not gone. I am. I quit. Tell them."

I want to say something that will last a lifetime, but what

can do that? What do I know? Shit—shit is what I know. At least that's what Uncle Beaner's told me in so many words. I'm a drop-out booking officer, a rum-bellied golfer who's not yet twenty-one and whose two iron tails, who can't just step up, test the breeze, and catch all of any shot anymore.

She backs out and weaves through the parking lot. Her brake lights come up at the stop sign, then she's on the street hurrying away. I hope she finds a place where people don't kill people.

Alison is gone, and Cool Breeze is dead. I hear about it two weeks after it's happened, and I think it's a rumor until I call Julio one day when he's working. He has the facts. Breeze was driving a van full of stereos, VCRs, TVs. He was shot. *How* is one fact Julio doesn't have.

I work, and I read, and I learn fifty ways to play solitaire on the computer. Every day Julio's put a note in my box. They say fact one, fact two, and so on. Fact one is Cool Breeze ran. I don't buy it. Breeze was not stupid. He'd have had his hands behind his head before he stepped out of the van, he'd lean up against it on his own, spread his legs before he was told, and he'd be talking the whole time, saying, *You see, officers, I am down on Fremont and a guy says* . . . Fact two is they say he had a gun. Not true. I know. Julio's facts are not telling me what happened.

I do sit-ups and I don't drink. My stomach's on its way back. I sharpen my game.

I turn twenty-one.

Another woman parole officer is run off the road and murdered. Again, Julio fills me in. Fact one is she drove her kids to a playground on a Saturday and didn't come home. Fact two is she'd been getting lilies in the mail.

It's a Sunday night when the phone rings at JuVee, and I'm thinking some parent is calling to see if we've got their kid. A man says, "Hey, brother, is Alison in?"

I say, "Alison quit."

"Alison, man," he says.

I say, "Long gone. She doesn't work here."

"The head lady in lock-up," he says. "She works nights. Bobbi's friend."

I say, "Is this Bobbi's husband?"

"No, man. Not Bobbi's husband."

I say, "Who is this?"

"I met Bobbi," he says. "Alison is gone?"

"From here and the state."

"Too bad," he says.

I say, "Do you want to talk to a supervisor?"

He says, "You got you a Lily working there?"

"No Lily," I say, and I'm dialing detention on another phone, trying to get someone in here.

"No Lily. That is sad. You need you a Lily."

The supervisor has picked up the phone and is saying, "Hello, hello?" I'm hoping he'll look in here. I say to the man, "I can get you a parole officer."

He says, "No Alison. No Lily. No Bobbi."

The supervisor has come to the small window in the door that leads to detention, and I wave him in. I mouth *killer* and point to the phone. To the man I say, "You're right. No Alison. No Lily and no Bobbi."

He says, "Only talk to Lily," and hangs up.

I tell the supervisor what he said, and we call the police. They say they'll send someone over, but I don't see anyone by quitting time, so I leave.

On the first tee at the DI, I hit a soft hook that takes the dogleg and leaves me half a seven iron to the green. You give me a seven iron and you might as well let me set the ball wherever I want. In my hands a seven iron's at least a birdie. The flag's at the back of the two-tiered green, and I go right at it. I start the round birdie birdie birdie and shoot a sixty-five.

The police come by my apartment in the afternoon. *Anything about the voice?* they say. *Young? Old? White? Black?*

"On something," I say.

"Drugs?"

"Something."

One of them says, "Definitely a man?"

"No question."

He says, "What did he say, exactly?"

I tell them he asked for Alison, and he said he'd met Bobbi.

"Met?" the cop says.

"He said, 'I met Bobbi.'"

The second cop says, "What else?"

"He asked if we had a Lily," I say. "He said we need a Lily, and he'd talk only to Lily."

The first cop says, "Did he threaten you?"

I say, "He said, 'No Alison. No Lily. No Bobbi.'"

"Did he say he'd hurt them?"

I say, "Only Alison is real."

"Real?"

"Bobbi is dead. There is no Lily."

We finish up, and they drive off. It's like I'm watching them pull away from the curb in a TV program. They think I'm a flake.

I didn't help. I want to help. I'd like to save a life. If I had to go to court and could, I'd look the guy in the eye and accuse him, if I'd seen him. He was cheerful. His voice had a lift to it as if he was smiling all the time.

He said to me, "No Alison. No Lily. No Bobbi."

I'd talked to a man who had murdered two women.

At three I call in and quit. The director tells me I can't. I owe them notice. I say, "Keep my check."

By midnight I'm in Tonopah, and I find a place to stay in the morning.

I can't locate anyone who has anything to do with the golf course they're supposed to be building here, and I don't see anyplace where they're putting one in. No heavy equipment, no dump trucks or bulldozers. When I do find someone, I'll show them the shots in my bag. I won't even hide my two iron. What will be between us is me knowing and them knowing that Tonopah, Nevada, will never get itself a real pro.

I went to Uncle Beaner with my song and dance because *one*, he's as filthy rich as Tosker L. Oddie was, and *two*, he's got a finger in every pie baked in the Silver State. *Three* is the real reason. My Uncle Beaner has kept alive his one daughter who is now my age and whose body doesn't feel pain. She bites pieces off her tongue, and only when her mouth fills with blood does she know it. Before Beaner learned to test her hot drinks, her lips were always blistered. Beaner or someone he's hired always has one eye on her. They tell her to shift her weight when she's standing, and they roll her when she sleeps. It was Beaner himself who one night threw her in his Caddi and drove eighty to Sunrise Hospital, and said, "Appendicitis." He swears he saw her stomach twitch under her blouse. They did the tests and operated. My point is he didn't abandon her on some hillside and hope for coyotes.

So, I took my best shot at Uncle Beaner. I gave him a floor show. I said, What's that? Can I sing? Can *I* sing. And I sang for him.

Tonopah is hot in the day and cold at night. In the morning I hit range balls into the desert, and I play twenty-one all afternoon. I rotate the Chinese exercise balls. They touch every finger, and I win more than I lose.

I am not a clown.

Uncle Beaner and my father, they'll come. As I said, Beaner has a finger in every pie, a snitch in every town and city and casino. They'll take the dips in the old highway and make the turn at what used to be the railroad spur at Sodaville. All the way they'll be cooking up one more bet I won't have the balls or smarts to turn down.

Halloween

I'm upstairs looking out the south dormer when two boys cut through our backyard. It's their shortcut to the junior high across the street. Downstairs our dog Maxine barks.

It's Halloween, and the boys are carrying sacks. One of them is Dracula in a high-collared black cloak. He has a toy shovel. The other boy, in a priest's collar, is slinging around a big silver crucifix. They act cocky. Dracula turns around and flashes a nice set of wax Dracula teeth. Maxine barks harder. She's a Doberman, and she is getting into her nasty act. It sounds like she's going to come through a window.

I sniff, and my nose begins to bleed. Always, first there is a stinging, like I've walked into something, then I sniff, and the blood comes.

I pinch my nose and start for the bathroom.

Helen, my wife, halfway up the stairs, is leaning over the banister. She's braided her hair into a loop, and I can see white scalp where the hair parts, marking the spot where someone might drive home a hatchet. Helen yells at Maxine, "Maxine, knock it off," then comes up, her head down, studying the steps as if there are footprints showing her where to put her feet. She stops, takes a hold of the railing and says, "Maxine, get a grip." Helen's braid swings.

I'm on the landing.

She sees me.

I stop.

She comes up, talking. She says, "*You* get a grip."

All day, Helen's been up and down the stairs every half

hour. She keeps looking at the ceiling, high into corners, the French maid hunting cobwebs and handling a duster.

I take one step down the stairs.

She circles around and is behind me. She puts her hands on my shoulders like I'm a steering wheel and says, "I'm not finished with you that you should be walking away." I try to sing *Gotta dance*, but it comes out like bad radio. Nasal. Adenoidal. I've squeezed my nose shut, and that's put a fist to my mouth. I've also brought a hand to my throat. I'm holding on.

Helen follows me down. She does my walk. She is doing my walk like it is a show business joke.

I step.

She follows up. She takes a step and says, "Stoop."

I step.

She steps and says, "Stoop. Stoop. Stoop." She says, "Don't stoop like you're a creature been born wrong." She has accused me of dowager's hump.

Maxine is at the bottom of the stairs. I can see she's got one bark left in her. Her mouth is all puckered up, and her eyes are popping out. It's like she's holding a toy she loves. I could knock her eyes off with a stick. I tell her if she doesn't let her bark go, she'll choke on it. Her ears slant like black butterflies.

Maxine and Helen stick to me, and we clog up the hall. I go into the bathroom, shut the door, and lean on the sink where blood drops and makes tiny red flowers. Helen says through the door, "Things can't go on like this." She's had to pick up her voice, and that's left her whiny. She says, "Something has to give."

She is not talking about the nosebleeds. They'll quit when they want to. She's talking about me not leaving the house. I go nowhere. Helen's thinking *shut-in*. She has the vocabulary for agoraphobia, but she's got me wrong. I can account for myself. When she nags, I put fingers to my temples, and I make my brow ardent. I give her what I can, one two three four. One, buzzards. Two, the sky appears to be falling. Three, outside is out of the frying pan into the fire. Four, every bush is a briar patch.

She says I'm singing in the wind and gives me some hard

facts. One, early retirement kills. Two, we're not rich. Three, What will the neighbors say?

Your family has one of me. We're the one you don't invite over. We live at your aunt's place or your grandparents'. The story is we won't budge. We're someone's child. A son. A daughter. But too old to be thought of in that way. We're your relative. Our name is Cal. Or, maybe something foreign. Maybe we're a Fredrika. Neighbors say we're dense. Bouts with scrofula have left us scarred. Could you get us to Thanksgiving dinner you wouldn't want us. We have no looks, and we forget our manners. Our thinking is dirty. Our hands won't stop. We talk with our mouths full and about ugly subjects.

I stand at windows, and I roam the house. Someone comes to the door, I answer it. I talk. I do polite things, but keep them on their side of the sill. I smile friendly like, and I say, Excuse me, and I put the door in their face.

Daily, I do push-ups, one foot over the other, my nose in and out of the diamond shape I've made with my hands.

Helen's prayer is, Keep him from dotage. She knows Pick's disease and Alzheimer's. Presenile dementia, she wonders. She reads medical columns and quizzes me, tests my short-term memory. I expect she'll one day pick through my scalp for dead brain cells. Her fear is I'm on my way to dodgy. Dodgy was her father. Helen stands where I sit. She is checking me out. Her father's eyes were sprung. He brought you in close and licked your ear.

Helen is still on the other side of the door. I hear her move like a pigeon. She knocks. Hers is a one-knuckle knock. It goes gnat-gnat.

I've got the faucet on, and I'm wetting tissue, going to put it under my upper lip to stop the bleeding.

She gives me gnat gnat once more.

I've got the tissue in, and I've tossed my head back. I cross my eyes. I say, "What?" It comes out *watt?* and sounds British.

I can't make out what Helen is saying. I think I hear her say *wood nut*. Wood nut as a question. Wood nut? Mumbo jumbo mumbo jumbo, wood nut?

I uncross my eyes and sniff. No blood. I wet a wash cloth and clean up my face.

Helen tries the knob. In the mirror, my eyes are gamy.

I turn on the floor heater, and it rattles like I've set beebees free on tin. The water is hot. I wet the cloth and squeeze it out. My hands burn. I put the cloth on my face the way barbers used to.

I'm in the early stages of something bad. I'm getting toothy. There's my puffed-out upper lip, and I've got body hair on my lower and upper back. If I turn sideways, you can see a hump between my shoulders. Someday it'll hatch some kind of beast. The nosebleeds come and go. The first one was five years back. I was forty-six. I woke up about 2 A.M. Had I heard a noise? Had a thing capable of it jostled the house? I sat up. I rumpled a blanket and reached for Helen. The stinging was there, like I'd taken a boxer's jab. I sniffed and blood came. Both nostrils. The first drop hit the sheet like a fat spider.

I clean up the sink and shut off the heater. When I come out Helen is not around. She isn't in the house. Maxine's at the end of the hall walking in circles. She swings in beside me, and we go to the bay window in the living room. Our car is taking the sway in the road that runs away from the house. At the corner, Helen turns left. She is going for Halloween candy. There is an empty platter on the stand by the front door.

A neighbor's truck comes up the road. It seems to have been hurled at us. The sun hits its windshield.

Helen has tied orange and black balloons around. They have witches in them. I bunt one. It flies away and comes back slowly, then hits another balloon and stops. Maxine stands up and puts her front paws on the window ledge. She looks to me for information.

On the front porch is a headless skeleton Helen bought. She's arranged cornstalks behind it and added a few pumpkins. You can plug the skeleton in. When you do, it swings a bony arm out front, presenting its skull like a waiter offering appetizers. The skeleton is asking if you want its skull. People have been pulling up and taking photographs for a week.

All summer the lilac bush on this side covers the house like a green cloud. This fall I didn't trim it. I should have cut it back in September. There will be fewer blossoms in the spring.

We buried our first cat under the lilac bush and marked the grave with a rock. We called him Roy. Helen spelled it R-o-i. Next to him is a black cat Helen found on the road. Out back over the years we've buried five dogs and a rooster. The rooster was a pet, like the dogs. We've buried maybe ten more cats there. We've even put cats under the marigolds that run along the driveway.

The nosebleeds come when the temperature drops, and we fire up the furnace. The doctor tells me the dry heat is the problem. I'm not to worry. Noses are bleeding all over the valley.

I don't sleep. Night comes, and I sit by the dormer. The earth hardens for winter, and the trees turn to stone. Our cats hunt mice. One named Egypt lines their bodies up on the patio where I find them in the mornings like tiny brown fish.

Sometimes I think I'm on the moon. The world is spent, and its truths are meager.

Up the road parents are letting kids out of cars. I bolt the front door.

Every day Helen makes calls in the downstairs bedroom. I see her in there, curled around the phone like a girl telling secrets to a doll. She calls our son and our daughter. She calls doctors and lawyers. She calls friends we've lost touch with. To all of them she says I am losing it. She says I'm nuts. I hear her.

She faces me when I look in. She says, "You're out of your brain." Our daughter writes. One letter follows another. She wants to know what is wrong with dad. Our son phones and asks for me. We talk. We say the things we should. He knows I watch the weather, so he looks that up and is ready with questions. He says, Dad? He says it like I might not actually be here.

Nuts is what Helen is doing to Maxine. It's Maxine's first season, and Helen is putting my jockey shorts on her. Helen's cut a hole for Maxine's tail. Her thinking is it's getting cold and Helen wants Maxine in the house as much as possible.

There's no getting Maxine out. Helen opens the screen and calls Maxine over. She says, "Need to make one?"

Maxine holds eye contact. The shorts hug her butt, and they're bloody, oranged.

"Make one?" Helen says.

Maxine sits down.

Helen says, "You don't want to, you don't have to." She shuts the screen, then pulls the door tight. Maxine whirls around, jumps up, and nips at Helen's hair. She catches a sleeve, and this delights her. She hops on her back legs while Helen takes her paws and says, "Puppy, puppy." Our dogs are lifelong puppies. Maxine throws herself at Helen, and Helen says, "Want a cook-eeeeee? Want an Orrrr-eeeeeee-o?"

Midnights, and I'm the one who is at the back door with Maxine, me in my shorts and Maxine in my shorts. She's whining. I'm working at the shorts she's wearing, and she is blowing air through her nose like a horse. She needs to go, but she won't. I say, "No choice." We stand there. I've got her bloody shorts off. I'm saying, "Out. Out. You have to." It's cold, but that's not the problem. The problem is it's a graveyard out back.

I take her collar and pull and shove until she tiptoes into the yard. She squats and keeps looking around like we're stealing fruit. Then she comes flying at me, and past, and I end up chasing her through the house. She's freewheeling, and I'm telling her she's got to get the shorts on.

I may be losing it. I may be nuts.

Idle hands, Helen says to me. She says, Idle hands, and turning sideways walks into other rooms. She comes up and takes my hands, and she says, The devil's workshop.

I sit by the dormer, and I see what comes out at night. The earth resists the loss of the sun. At my feet, an amaryllis grows in a pot. Egypt brings home her mice. Maxine knows I am up. I hear her downstairs walking the halls, afraid of the stairs. She won't climb them. She does her stern circles down there.

Helen makes her calls, and I make mine, out in the open, at the phone by the front door. I call radio talk shows. I keep the volume up so they say to me, "Shut off your radio. We're on a delay." I say, "What?" They get mad. Can't you hear them off mike? *Some idiot,* they are saying. They give me the finger. Can you see them seeing red?

This morning the host of "The Garden House" said, "Firm up your voice." We were waiting to go on the air.

I said, "What? Firm up my voice?"

"Firm up your voice," he said.

"What?" I said.

He said, "You're quavering."

I said, "Quavering?"

"Quavering," he said.

I hung up, and I turned off the radio. Maxine came over. I took her face in my hands. What they don't understand is that I deserve their service.

Helen isn't going to make it back in time with the candy. Some kids out front are pointing at the skeleton, then punching each other. There are a couple of teenagers and five children, five little ghosts. It's probably a family. One of the teenagers is a Ninja. He's in black and has a white sweatband around his forehead. It's got a red circle on it. The other big kid is a green monster. He's working on the bloody stub of an arm that comes out of his jacket when he pulls something in his pocket.

Special effects. These kids understand special effects. They admire them.

I can give them special effects. I start with my sweater. I take it off.

The Ninja does some kicks. You can tell he knows what he is doing. His feet and hands strike like darts. Wouldn't that be something? To be so quick and powerful you could put your fist through some guy's chest and be about to take his heart into your hand before he knows he's been hit.

I'm down to my jockey shorts and my t-shirt, and the trick-

or-treaters are coming up the porch steps. Helen is too late. It's dusk. I turn on the overhead light and unbolt the door.

They're on the porch, and they're laughing at Helen's skeleton. These kids are fearless. One of the ghosts reaches for the skeleton's skull.

I have a treat for them. They won't believe it. I pull off my t-shirt, and I call Maxine over. She's been at the window, not barking, but growling deep in her throat.

What's behind this door is me and Maxine in jockey shorts. Here is my body. Its torso has gone to slag. It's titted. It's matted with black hair that looks like a hillside after a brush fire.

I open the front door. There's still a screen door between me and the kids. The stinging comes. I sniff, and the blood flows, both barrels, heavy and pitiless.

Maxine sounds like hell.

I'm pushing open the screen door. I won't have to say boo.

Union Business

Of all people Rita, my mother, has hold of my sleeve like a carny barker, and she's hustling me, her sloppy red lips saying, "What will it cost you?"

We're in the corridor outside my office in the Telmac Building where the union owns the third floor. She's bent me like a safety pin, and her mouth is filling my ear with words. We're the picture of shtick, her yakking and me spilling the coffee I just got and walking in it. She says, "What's the price? An hour? Maybe two, or God forbid three."

I coax and steer, get her inside, wave at the couch, and say, "Won't you sit?"

She takes the chair by my desk.

"Coffee?" I say. Mine's sloshed onto me, and there are reddish spots the color of blood on the carpet and a trail of them up the hallway.

She says, "Hills Brothers."

This from the woman who taught me coffee is coffee, and life is not a merry-go-round.

"Never mind," she says and shifts and creaks.

The Kleenex I'm using to dry my hands is breaking up.

Rita has these tiny dinosaur arms, and she fusses with things. How she got here I don't know. She can drive but won't, and I can't see her on a bus.

She's up and has my sleeve again, and we're stumbling past the desk. The Venetian blinds are open. She grabs the cord, yanks them toward the ceiling, and says, "Out there, look." She pins me to the glass. We're six stories up. Outside, the Las

Vegas heat's a killer. It's baking the asphalt, and the blue mountains toward L.A. shimmy on the horizon. When we were boys, me and my friends, we'd fry eggs on car hoods.

Rita says, "What I drove down here is over there. I got in behind the steering wheel, put a key in, turned it and pumped the gas, backed out, and I was able to come here across the city at great risk." One of her hands does half a flip, dismissing it all as poppycock. "Visitors is where I parked," she says.

She's not in the visitors lot. Rita can park in the lobby if she wants to.

I go to get her coffee.

She won't sit. She'll put-put around my office on a slant and stop every three steps like she's hit a logjam I'm somehow the reason for. Rita can be a real tugboat.

Her point in coming is to ask what it will cost me to see the new house she and Dick Handy bought.

You call my father Dick Handy, both names, not Richard or Dick, not Mr. Handy. You say, *Dick Handy, good to see you.* The men he is union president over, you hear them say, *Dick Handy, how's it hanging?* And he says, *Handy.* He pokes his handshake at you until you take it, and when you do, he reels you in, squeezes your shoulders together and says, *Still hitting the back of the urinal?*

One day a man who works for Dick Handy told me Dick Handy is strong enough and willful enough that if he chose to kill himself he could do it by hurling his own body against whatever floor he was standing on.

Rita won't take her coffee, and I end up spilling it on my desk. I say, "Secretary says it's Hills Brothers," and she says, "Black?"

"Please," I say. "Won't you sit?"

She drags me back to the window and says, "It's a hop off the freeway, and two lefts and a right." She unclips the pen from my shirt pocket and on a folder marks out streets and labels them. "It's a hop, skip, and a jump," she says. She tells me what speeds to travel and when to change lanes.

They live in El Dorado Estates. She writes that in Spanish-looking letters.

She says, "Tell your mother you're a good boy."

I tell Rita I'm a good boy, and I say I will come by on the way home.

I say, "Let me see you out."

"I'm not dumb," she says.

The El Dorado Estates security people almost salute me. The gate's wheeled out of my way, and I don't even slow down. Rita's on the sidewalk in front of their place. She looks rickety and hot. I'm not yet out of the car when she says, "Jan is bringing the boys over." Jan is my wife, and the boys are Nick and James. Nick is fourteen, and James is sixteen. Rita holds onto to me, and we trip our way up a row of cement circles to the porch.

Inside, she points me to where Dick Handy is and says, "Surprise him."

He's got a game show on, and it's loud. There is something edgy about the way he sits in his leather chair. He's in an aviator's jumpsuit and has unzipped it down the front. The neck of his t-shirt shows. He's rolled his socks down so they're dark bracelets around his ankles, and he is holding a tall plastic mug. He's drinking whiskey, Wild Turkey. I can smell it.

He comes up out of his chair and jerks me in so we're stuck together. I'm six-four, and I feel puny. He says, "The Long-of-It," and stops a fist half an inch short of my stomach. I'm The-Long-of-It, or I'm The-Thin-Man. Dick Handy's not the short of it. He is six-seven. To him, I'm skinny and smart. He'll rub his scalp and say, "Meet Thick," and then get me in a friendly hammerlock and say, "Meet the Brain behind the Brawn." Out on Lake Mead, at a driving range, jammed into our seats at a UNLV game, over and over, he tells me about some TV show they used to do where a jock and a brain team up. The jock kicks a field goal or buries ten free throws. Maybe he sinks a putt, and the brain answers tough questions. Dick Handy claims we can ace a show like that.

We stand here focused on the set.

He says, "Idiots."

On TV two men in ugly suits and a woman who seems to have pin cushions on each shoulder answer statements with questions. The host is serious-eyed, and he's got baroque hair. I think he's some old rock-and-roll star.

Dick Handy pours me some rum he keeps around, rattles the ice, and, passing me the glass, says, "Pussy." He drinks from his mug. "You could do this," he says and points his drink at the game show. He says, "Look how far their heads are up their asses."

We sit down, him on the edge of his chair and me on the edge of mine, both of us up on our toes. Shoot off a gun, and we'd do a hundred yards fast.

"You can answer these questions with your hands tied behind your back," Dick Handy says. "You can do this blindfolded." The cloth belt attached to his jumpsuit is unbuckled, and its ends hang like possum.

I sip my pussy drink, lean back, relax.

Dick Handy, when he's doing union-president business, wears all-cotton white shirts. They're long-sleeved no matter how hot Vegas is and lightly-starched, and his slacks are dry-cleaned after he puts them on and takes them off. Sometimes he changes six times a day. His shoes are Florsheim and are taken every Friday to a shop off Fremont Street to be polished. He buys ties like candy bars. Dick Handy's men wouldn't know him in a jumpsuit.

According to Dick Handy, where physical work comes in I have two speeds, slow and slower. He tells me, *Your brains, for them you thank Rita.* She writes all his personal letters.

One of the idiots on TV says, "What are monozygotic twins?"

Rita comes in carrying a bowl and says, "I phoned the gate, and they'll sail Jan right through. I described her and your boys." Rita gives me the bowl and a fork. "Try it," she says. "Dessert first."

I finish my rum and get up. The fork swings in the bowl. "What is this?" I say.

"Try it," Rita says.

We walk toward the kitchen, and I stab at some kind of frozen ice-cream cake.

Rita tells me she ordered pizza and Chinese.

The cake spurts up the side of the bowl and almost out.

We hear Dick Handy behind us. "I'll show you around," he says. His concentration is on the TV.

"In a minute," Rita says, and she grabs the bowl from me, opens the microwave, puts the dessert inside and taps a button. She says, "It's better kind of melted, soft. Thirty seconds is all it needs."

I say, "Pizza," and lick the fork. "The boys will love you."

"Pizza," she says. "Chinese for Dick Handy. Your boys, they owe me."

"Owe you?"

"And Jan. How long since we've seen our grandsons. They're grown men by now, right? What—they can't drive? A boy sixteen in this modern world doesn't have a license to drive a car? And their mother?"

"I owe you," I say. "Not Jan, not the boys."

The microwave buzzes.

Rita says, "Get that."

The dessert is spongy, and it tastes like cherries and graham crackers.

The only thing about Dick Handy at sixty-three that is not what it was when he was twenty is his hearing. The TV is as loud as it might be in a football stadium. When a commercial comes on, he punches the sound off, and you think you've been dunked under water.

Rita says she has things to tell me about Dick Handy I don't want to hear.

I tell her I've heard enough things I don't want to hear.

She says, "Dick Handy lies."

The sound drops on the TV, and we hear Dick Handy say, "You got to see this. Come here. Get in here." Then he turns it up and yells at the idiots. They're pinheads, all of them.

What Rita doesn't understand is that sons know fathers lie.

She says, "Here's a hypothetical. Suppose, what if Dick Handy and your mother are out on the boat he bought so the family could be together more. We're on Lake Mead, just me and Dick Handy, and a storm blows in which no one could have told us was coming. No weather report, and it's on top of us. It makes waves big as houses. It knocks us out of the boat and into the water. And suppose the boat—what? When it turns over and sinks—what is that?"

"The boat capsizes," I say, washing my bowl at the sink.

She says, "Yes," and takes the bowl from me. She says, "We have a dishwasher."

I take the dishtowel she gives me and dry my hands.

She says, "The boat flips over and goes under the water like a rock. What's left is only one oar, and the laws of the way the world is say if we both use it we'll die. We'll sink and come up days later like old couches. Do you think Dick Handy would leave it for me and go under himself?"

I'd argue that more than an oar would be left, I'd say that you don't get on Dick Handy's boat unless you're wearing a life jacket, but this is one of Rita's hypotheticals, and I say, "Dick Handy would die for you."

"No," Rita says, and she lays her head back, lays it back in a way that has always made clouds gather. Her throat, I see, is egg-white.

"He'd save you both," I say. "He's smart and that strong."

She says, "Now, in this day and time, what union business is there at eleven and twelve at night? You tell me. You're a big shot, an office next to your father. Where is Dick Handy going at night until three and four in the morning when he's sixty-three years old and should be here with your mother? Are you out, away from your Jan and boys at four A.M.?"

What can I say to her? Dick Handy's union is the one I am a lawyer for, but his union is not mine. He sent me to Cal, and the result was a B.A. and a master's. Then he paid for Berkeley, and I'm a lawyer and a CPA. My office *is* next to his. But Dick Handy's union is the one you see in movies. At a Thanksgiving dinner, years ago, the woman my brother married said, "What

I liked about the Godfather movies was that you knew where you stood. They had rules, and you did what you had to do, and if you didn't do what the rules said, if you did something not in the rules, what happened to you was clear and settled beforehand, maybe even that you die, a bullet to the head, and you knew it. You took the result that was coming to you." What she described—that is Dick Handy's union.

I hug Rita, and I say, "Union business is what he is doing."

"He tells me that," she says. I see for the first time her eyes are grave and her hair is ash.

"It's true," I say.

She says, "He lies."

"Not to you."

She backs up, crying. She is saying, "I ask him to his face— and I'm not blinking, I'm not mealymouthing this, I ask, 'What specific union business keeps its president out until the sun comes up in the morning?' I say, 'Give me details I can believe.' And he says, 'What did I tell you?'"

On the refrigerator behind Rita is a sticker from the Heart Institute of Nevada. It shows the outline of a telephone, and pasted on top of it is a man who is hunched over. His hands are digging for his heart. His heart's a squirrel inside him that has cut loose in eight directions at once. Underneath, in red letters, it says, CHEST PAIN HOTLINE 731–0000.

We hear the TV shut off and are looking at Dick Handy when he comes in the kitchen. He tips fresh Wild Turkey into his mug, then stops and stands here like a wind-up toy. You'd think a firecracker has blown away his eyebrows and eyelashes. He says, "A knucklehead with false teeth and a cheap toup won fifteen thousand dollars for saying 'What is the Red River Valley?'"

"Song?" I say.

"Close," he says. He taps my head. He pours more Wild Turkey and says, "You know how I was circumcised?"

"God," Rita says. She picks up some dishcloths and walks out on us.

How Dick Handy was circumcised is one story I haven't heard.

"What they did," he says, and he raises his mug, sips then gulps and comes out of it smacking his lips and overdoing an *ah*. He's getting his timing down. He says, "What they did was they soaked a cotton ball in whiskey—most likely Wild Turkey—and put it in your mouth—you being me the baby—and they started cutting, leaving you on your own, doing your damnedest to get into your first serious drunk."

I believe him.

Rita calls from a back room. "Jan'll be here in ten minutes." A dryer is spinning, and something is clicking in it.

Dick Handy says, "Come see this alarm system," and he guides me to the stairs that lead to the bedrooms. I count eight surveillance cameras in two rooms, and there is one stuck to the ceiling at the top of the stairs. We go up. He flips on a switch and says, "Try sneaking in at night, put one foot on the first step, and you're dead. If I don't get you, an army is here in three minutes. I've timed them." There is a red light on under the camera's lens. All the cameras have red lights.

I say, "How does it know the good guys from the bad guys?"

"Everyone's a bad guy," he says and turns off the switch.

I admire the new model cars he's put together. They run on genuine rubber tires. Their trunks open and close. The hoods come off.

We end up on the back patio where, as he's already told me, the yard's no bigger than a handball court, and it's all flagstone and cement. There are two trees in three-by-three-foot boxes of dirt. The yard's fenced, a six-foot cinder block wall all around, and oleanders and pyracantha shrubs border the flagstone. There is a surveillance camera on a post in each corner. Their old house had a pool.

"Swimming?" I say.

Dick Handy'd die if he didn't get his swim in every morning. He tells me there is a spa half a block away, an Olympic-sized pool for laps and a diving pool. You see Dick Handy swim and you understand how the Egyptians built the pyramids. He does a stubborn crawl he can keep up hour after hour.

His bird-watching scope is set up on a redwood table. He goes over, leans so he can see, turns a knob and adjusts the angle.

We sit on a redwood bench.

A month before they bought this house, Rita called me at work and said Dick Handy was shooting up the neighborhood. She said, "He shot at a cat. He's in the street like it's Dodge City, and he's firing a gun, for God's sake."

I had Jan meet me, and she sat with Rita, who said, "He pointed it at me."

Dick Handy was out back by the pool, sitting at the wrought iron table where he and his friends played poker. To see them at it was to see Zeus and his boozy council on a day off.

I sat down and said, "How's it hanging?"

"Handy," he said.

I said, "What's up?"

The pistol sat on the table, and there was a phone on the chair next to him. He'd set up the birding scope. He adjusted the focus, swung the scope around, and bent over to look in it. He kept a notebook of the birds he saw. In it, he'd write down the names of the birds, where he spotted them, and the dates. I saw two new entries, a black-chinned hummingbird and a broad-tailed hummingbird. For place, he'd written *backyard*.

"It's a .22, not a gun," he said. "Put it between my eyes and pull the trigger. It goes off, and I get up and mow the lawn. That's how much of a gun it is." He offered me the scope.

Jan could have come out of the house, her arm around Rita's waist, and, as the loving daughter-in-law, said, "Dad, talk to us."

Not me. My role was to sit here.

He aimed the .22 at one of the hummingbird feeders he'd hung out, closed one eye and said, "Bang bang."

He once asked me what hummingbirds sound like. Their pitch is too high for Dick Handy. He can hear men talk, but not all women. I said, "They whirr. You can feel and hear it. A vibration."

He touched my throat, his fingers open as if he was reaching for a book, and said, "Say it."

I said, "Whirrrrrrring," and I could feel it in the tips of his fingers.

That day, the day Rita called to say Dick Handy was shooting up the neighborhood, Dick Handy and I sat by the pool until dark. Hummingbirds sucked at his feeders. They had throats as rosy as desert sunsets. Finally, the phone rang, and Dick Handy picked it up. He listened, then he calmly lowered the phone to his lap. He said, "Motherfuckers."

Now I sit here again in his new house's backyard, and the table is redwood. The birding scope is here. You'd think you could fold it up and unfold it like one of those toys that turns from a car into a hero then back again. People who meet Dick Handy, but who don't really know him, ask him how he is, and he wants to pull their ears off.

No one does Dick Handy's errands. Every day he's at the wheel of his own car, and he buys his own clothes, the white shirts and the three-hundred-dollar pants. At six-foot-seven, he's not lost an inch and is broad-chested and handsome. His white hair swirls like tumbling water, and he keeps his mouth clamped shut. When he eats, he chews silently. He's in his office when he needs to be.

A few feet away from us, a bird lands on one of the trees, and Dick Handy, squinting into the scope, points at it. He writes on his pad and hands it to me. It says, Northern Bullock's Oriole, and he's written *female*, plus the date and the location, which is *new backyard*. He turns the scope for me, and I fumble around trying to find the bird in it. When I do, I see it has a yellow chest and a narrow stripe on its wing. Another bird flies in and slips through the branches toward the female. It's jittery and goes *kleak kleak*. Then it jumps her.

The bird is done before I can say *what?*, and I look at Dick

Handy, who says, "Gave her a little poke." He says. "That s. of a b. deflowered her."

Rita and Jan are coming out of the house, Nick and James in front carrying the cartons of Chinese, the boxes of pizza, and the ill-temper that defines their teenage lives. They stop. They're dumbstruck bystanders.

I'm in tears, laughing, and I'm swinging my arms for balance because I'm falling off the redwood bench, and Dick Handy is not far behind. He's grabbing the table to keep from hitting the flagstone. They don't understand what they didn't hear, which was Dick Handy saying, "Do you think she had time for an organism?"

Jan moves in. She says, "What?"

"Don't ask," Rita say. "It's dirty whatever it is."

After passing around knives and forks, trading plates, filling glasses, nit-picking, we've split up. Nick and James are left at the redwood table, and Rita and Jan have gone inside. They're in the kitchen. I'm with Dick Handy on the patio. Dick Handy hasn't put down his mug of Wild Turkey. The late evening sun lights up his forearms, and it looks like there is a tiny brush fire on each one. He could have been an athlete, a football player, a power forward—a pro, not just a college jock. He was—he is—quick to go along with his big. But he got himself hired to build houses when he was thirteen. He lifted and picked up, then was a hod carrier and laid bricks, framed, poured concrete. We've got black-and-white photographs of him and the men he worked with, all of them with their shirts off, black from the sun, the white band of their shorts showing above their pants and matching their teeth.

I toss my pizza in a trash can and say, "What about golf?" Dick Handy plays scratch.

"Not here," he says, and he waves at the golf course on the other side of the fence. He says, "What is that—a golf course? I don't think so. See any trees? I've played Augusta, don't forget. Pebble Beach."

I say, "And the Harley?"

"Gave it to Shirley's kid." Shirley is a sheet metal man Dick Handy started out working with.

Dick Handy owned this Harley as big as an elephant. He'd ride it over to Bullhead City and up to the Grand Canyon. He'd put on his Harley cap, kind of a yaughtman's hat with Harley wings on the front and blue braid across the bill.

I tell him I'm going for dessert and ask if he wants some.

He says, "I'll make do," and lifts his mug.

Inside, Jan and Rita are sitting at the dinner table. They've crossed their legs and are talking like high school girls.

I say to Rita, "You telling Jan things she doesn't want to hear?"

Jan says, "There's nothing I don't want to hear."

I pull the dessert out of the refrigerator, and Rita says, "Put it in the microwave."

Jan says, "Take it outside."

"Fathers lie," I say.

"Ain't that God's truth," Jan says.

Rita says, "Oh God, yes."

Should I tell them I've been told Dick Handy has killed at least one man. There's a guy whose friend knows a man who saw Dick Handy shoot a California highway patrolman in the head. The man and Dick Handy were doing some union business.

Dick Handy is standing by the back fence, his arms on top of it. His mug's by his elbow. I go over and rest against the cinder blocks a few feet away. I'm eating my second bowl of dessert.

On the day I was married, Dick Handy held me the way fathers hold sons on a greeting card and said, "Work and believe in God." He tapped his head with a knuckle and poked my stomach and said, "Me and you, Thick and Thin. Brains, you've got. Use them."

I did.

He is muscle, and I am bone.

Now, here by the fence, he says, "I'm an old man who

watches the news, and I live in the desert where I do things I believe in. I do my work, I keep the union where it needs to be, and I continue to believe in God."

I say, "Come on. Let's go annoy the women."

He gulps Wild Turkey and smacks his lips. He spreads his legs. He says, "'Beware the pine tree's withered branch. / Beware the—'" He can't find the words. They aren't here. He says, "'Beware the'—the what? The . . . da da da . . . the something something." He lifts his mug to his forehead and says, "'Beware the'—God, I'm thick."

When I was a boy, he'd do "The Shooting of Dan McGrew" and act it out. It'd be like he had six-guns on. He'd go slack-jawed and crack a wily grin and say, "'A bunch of boys were whooping it up in the Malamute Saloon; / The kid that handles the music-box was hitting a jag-time tune.'" Dick Handy'd be the boys whooping it up and the kid hitting the jag-time tune. He stomped and stamped, slid along the carpet, turned and beat out the tune on his thighs. He sang, "'Back at the bar, in a solo game, sat Dangerous Dan McGrew, / And watching his luck was his light-o'-love, the Lady known as Lou.'"

Here, on the flagstone, he bounces on his toes. He's kept his feet apart and is a boxer who's telling you to take your best shot. He can slip anything you throw. No one can touch him, not even the knockout punch that has been coming for a longtime from God only knows what direction.

Two nights from tonight, he'll get a phone call at eleven. He'll get out of his jumpsuit and into one of his white shirts, and he'll drive off. He'll tell Rita it's union business, and her last words to him will be, "What union business can't wait until tomorrow?" She'll pick up the phone to call me, think about Dick Handy saying, "What did I tell you?", and she won't push the one button programmed to ring my number.

The police will find his body a week later in a three-foot grave on this side of Sunrise Mountain, and they'll think I want to hear the details of what they found, how his hands were tied behind his back, how he was blindfolded and shot once right between the eyes. Whoever did it shoved a red deer tag up his naked ass.

I am fifteen, it's summer, and I am driving Dick Handy to Needles, California. I'm holding his restored and modified Jaguar under seventy. We've cranked the top down, and I'd say Dick Handy is happy. He's your image of the man in *Look* from the fifties. We're wearing shades, and we've got on these gag cowboy hats we bought at a rest stop.

I can't tell you much about me. I think I'm working on a ducktail.

It's nineteen sixty-two, and this is a journey.

Dick Handy tells me to bet on the Dodgers, and he talks about the time his Cessna iced up and tried to dump him into the Grand Canyon.

Then he doesn't talk. His arms are behind his head and fanned out, and if he smoked you'd see a fat cigar in his face and his white teeth nibbling at it.

I sneak the Jag up to seventy-five. We're on a two-lane highway.

Dick Handy says, "What do women want?"

I touch my nose, start to say what I think.

"Don't answer," he says. "It's a rhetorical question."

One Christmas Rita gave Dick Handy a gold letter opener she'd ordered for him. It had a complicated geometric leaf and flower design on the handle, and he carried it around for a week, touching things and people, blessing them. You didn't ask why or what.

I've got us doing eighty.

He says, "Someday you'll want to know what women want. You'll come to Dick Handy on your knees, and you'll say, 'Tell me. What do women want?' You'll be married, and I'll tell you, and you won't listen, not even then, not even then when you really want to know."

I'm doing eighty-five, and I feel something behind my eyes that says this may be the best moment of my life. I say, "Hit me with it." I put a finger gun to my forehead, and I say, "Right between the eyes."

He says, "Hit you with it," and Dick Handy places his hands on the dashboard. His wedding ring is Indian, silver with black and red and turquoise triangles. On his right hand is a ring for being president of the Lions Club. He says, "Right here, here in this desert where it's probably one hundred and ten degrees, and there is all this dirt and nothing else, you can hear it. Right now. And at night, when it's quiet, it's deafening. You can hear it in big cities and small towns, in restaurants, where it's crowded and noisy, dishes and haggling and eating. You can hear the women chanting."

He takes off the silly toy cowboy hat and raises himself up in his seat. He cups a hand behind each ear like he is listening. The wind blows his hair. He's timing his punch line. Here's where the sixty-three-year-old Dick Handy would sip Wild Turkey like he'd been assigned the job of thinking about what the world needs in order to save itself.

Back in his seat, he turns toward me and sets his hands so they're about ten inches apart. He could be telling me a fish story. He says, "Hear it. They're saying, Dick. They're chanting, We want dick. We want dick."

And I can't help it. I almost wreck the Jaguar, rip it into, then out of, a soft shoulder. He's told me the craziest thing in the world you can tell a fifteen-year-old boy who is hurling a forty-thousand-dollar car through the Arizona desert at one hundred miles an hour.

We drive to a church in Needles, one being built, and he has me park in a corner of the lot away from the building and at an angle across the parking slots that have been painted in. There are three trucks near a side entrance. He gets out, leaving his door open, and says, "I'll be fifteen minutes."

In the street, a kid is teaching a dog to run down a tennis ball and bring it back. I get caught up in their game and don't see Dick Handy until I focus on him in a doorway talking to a man who is taller than he is. The man's body says he's upset. I see Dick Handy raise both hands up like he's saying *relax*, and then he swings, and the man goes down. The man tries to get up, makes it to one knee, and Dick Handy hits him again, slams him into the sidewalk. I find myself amazed that Dick Handy is left-handed. He hits the man all the way into the parking lot, pile-driving lefts, over the top and down. You'd have to be running all out in a pitch-black night and smack into a brick wall to understand the power behind one of Dick Handy's blows. Five men have come out of the church, and they're standing around, touching their tool belts, their hammers. Dick Handy walks back to them, singles each one out, and says something. Then he is in the car, and we are driving away, and he says, "Those sons of pups."

We drive to a school yard, where he has me stop, and we get out and walk two blocks to a Mexican diner. He's greeted like he's come home. A square-faced Mexican he calls Jake grips Dick Handy, and they tug at each other until Jake's wife, Marta, reaches out, kisses Dick Handy on the cheek, and says, "Too long, Dick Handy. Too long." She walks us to a table, and Dick Handy heads for the restroom. When he gets back, he sits next to me in the booth. His hand's wrapped in a towel. He leans in close to me and says, "Don't ever let these people see that you drive a Jaguar."

A girl my age takes our order. She is Jake and Marta's daughter, Marti. Her hair is black and thick and lively and is pulled to one side up over her ear. Dick Handy introduces me. He says to her, "Be careful of his kind. They know what women want."

He orders soup and rice for us and tells me if I order beans I walk home to Vegas. After Marti has brought our food, he says, "Some advice from your father. Two items from Dick Handy's book on how to live. One, you judge a place by its soup. Here is the best soup in California, Arizona, and Nevada put together. Two, never set your cap for a girl until you've seen her mother. You see her mother, and you see your bride in twenty years. Fat, thin, mean, kind, good bad ugly, you name it."

I say, "Set your cap?"

"Set your cap, smart ass," he says. "Fifteen and you're a smart ass and too pussy to try the hot sauce."

I punch a chip into the hot sauce and eat the whole thing in one bite. It's a mistake. My eyes sting, and I've burned the roof of my mouth.

"Pussy," Dick Handy says.

I slap my tongue on the burn, and there are tears in my eyes. "Water," I say.

"Set your cap," he says and hands me a plastic water pitcher. "Courting, you know. Dating, wanting to marry. What's your word?"

I finally kill the hot sauce. "Hustle," I say.

He unwraps the towel. There is blood on his finger where his ring's cut it. He wipes the blood off, then cocks his head. He's listening. Someone is calling him. He puts his hurt hand behind his ear and cups it. Blood has dried on his wrist. He says, "Hear it? Even here, right here in all this noise. In all this unholy racket. Dick, they're saying. We want dick. Dick dick dick. All the wives, and the daughters, all the girls."

My Home State of Nevada

She put the door in my face. I was coming in, and she was coming out. The door was glass. She said, "Thank you." But she'd done the work.

The birthmark on her neck looked like my home state of Nevada.

So, I followed.

I galloped.

I said, "*Wie geht's?*"

She studied the sidewalk, me and my chutzpa, the jay-bird-blue sky, the oleanders behind us. She said, "*Trés bien,*" and an orange cat slinked by.

I thought, A multilingual family.

I could have said, I could have said, I could have said, and if I had, she'd have raised a curtain of anger. I said, "God, I'm hungry. Lunch?"

We ate. We had children. They spoke Chinese, Portuguese, Pontiac, French, Russian, and German. They went away, and they became Mormons.

With each birth her birthmark diminished until it was a red dot the shape of Lake Mead. She had it lasered, and one day it wasn't here. Layer by layer, I undid the bed, I combed the furrowed ground of the garden she'd worked row by row, I flashlight-swept the shag carpet square foot by square foot, noodle by noodle.

What was gone was lost.

My home state of Nevada had a run of luck. Mount Oddie rained silver ore on Tonopah, the sagebrush gave way and coats of grass rolled in, the rivers gained depth and width, and every Christmas snow fell on Las Vegas, my hometown.

We moved to Sparks near enough to Reno and burned our bridges and rode taxis. Money was no object.

Her hair leapt left and right from a part down the middle. We got on. We did.

The lean years came, as they do, and we sat in Windsor chairs and looked fixedly at the blue mountains and the dirt or we quarreled. Too often, it was *me first! me first!* first thing in the morning.

Our oldest became a prophet.

We saw him on TV. His lips were wet, and he looked benign.

We zigzagged across the Great Basin without telling anyone when we expected to return, not because we felt like tin gods or jackanapes or back-talking kids. We showed our respect. We didn't skimp on water, we kept our clothes on, and we did not put our feet or hands in places we couldn't see. Once she did sit down without looking, and I prepared myself to suck venom from her wounds wherever they might be.

We found a cave in Montana where you sit and absorb radon gas. We paid to get in and we sat and played hearts. There had been published disagreement. The scientists said we would die. The locals said we were cured.

She said, "In whom should we trust?", and the sun smacked us as we emerged.

Nothing Sad, Once You Look at It

The way I saw it Francie was flying the coop, was leaving for reasons she was not willing to put in plain English. I fussed around and said *What did I do? What did I do?* until she covered her ears and showed me her back. Not that she just up and left, and she wasn't pissed. From the get-go she was straight with me and laid out what little she had of a plan.

"But," I said, "you won't say why."

She told me I had it wrong.

"How?" I wondered.

She said, "Just do."

Like when I asked why her boy in California didn't have a phone, and she said, "He doesn't have a phone." Now his having a phone or not having a phone was none of my business, and she could have said that, but the subject came up, and I asked a simple question. Her answer wasn't an answer, and I said so. I said, "What's his reason?", and she said, "He doesn't have a phone because he doesn't have a phone."

True is true. God is good, and a lie is a lie. You yourself, you've been around her kind of thinking, know someone who can add two to any number and come up with four. Don't cross the street. Why? Just don't cross the street. Scissors cuts paper, paper covers rock, rock breaks scissors. Easy as that.

So Francie was flying the coop because Francie was flying the coop. Nothing could stop her. "Not even yours truly," I said to her, and she said, "You got that right." Not mean, but direct in-your-face honesty.

I said, "What if I sang your praises?"

"I'd like that."

"Shackled you to something?"

She flexed for me and said, "Strong enough?"

I said, "Nothing'll stop you."

"Nothing."

We talked it to death.

The upshot was her leaving grew into a god-given stubborn fact.

But Monday was news.

Her telling me she was going on Monday fell out of the sky and hit me hard as the law. Up until the minute she spoke the word *Monday* her going for good was only a bad thought.

We'd gone to Lions Park where we sat and ate Kentucky Fried Chicken we had picked up on our walk over. I polished off my box and part of Francie's and was wiping down with one of those wet cloths she always had around, had it slapped to my face when Francie sat back and said, "Monday is the day I'll be going."

"This Monday coming up?" I said. I talked through the wet cloth, and my voice came out weak and sneaky. I felt small.

She said, "The one coming up."

It was Thursday, and me and Francie and our dog, Bloom, were about the only living things in the park. There were some boys from the junior high across the street goofing off near a playground, kicking up dust and grabassing on the monkey bars. They looked like bears in someone's camp. *Insolent* jumped to mind. From where I didn't know. Put something in front of me and I'd read it, so words stuck. These boys had the world by its tail. One of them flipped a swing up as high as it would go to see if he could get it to come down on the wrong side. It curled up, then fell back toward him, and the other boys hooted and smacked him around.

Francie said, "It's for your good, in some ways." She picked up a twig, and her eyes dove inside her.

If I'd've said *Why?*, she'd've said, *It's not that I won't tell you. It's that I don't know. Why is not clear to me. But having to go is.*

That's capital-t truth from a woman with a college degree. Go figure, right?

I said, "But mostly for your good, right?"

"Mostly mine," she said. Francie was a woman who said straight out what she had to say. She'd put her hair up in a ponytail, and it shot out like a kid's drawing of sprinkler water. It made her young. You've seen pictures of girls doing ballet. Francie looked like one of those fourteen-year-olds, like one of those long skinny girls sitting on a hardwood floor, one leg straight out and the other one tucked up under their butt, their satin shoes off. Francie looked like she'd just come in from putting her face in the rain.

I dumped our cups and napkins and slugged down the last of our root beer. Francie fed Bloom chicken, picking out the bones so he didn't choke on one. She gave her empty box to me, and I tossed it. She took my arm the way she did, the way you'd hold onto a live bird, and she said, "I'll miss softball." Her ponytail sprinkled up and out behind her. She said, "All you men so full of it and having serious fun. Hitting homers and playing pepper where that sign says No Pepper Here."

Should I have been a wet blanket and said, *Then why are you flapping your wings like some big bird and taking off?* Should I have dropped to the ground, rolled back and forth, yanked out hair, and beat my chest? When I was little, and I'd throw a tantrum, my grandmother'd say, "Go sit on thorns."

The house we rented was two streets from the park and an easy walk. Bloom ran ahead of us. He had this way of trotting that said he was a jock who'd just hit a key field goal. He waited at the front gate. I kicked around the yard, and Francie called in an ad for the TV and dryer she'd bought. I'd told her to sell the washer I'd paid for. She had said, "No way. It's yours." I mowed and swept, and she took Bloom to the market for eggs and came back with a carful of groceries. Like some heart-of-gold woman, she wasn't leaving her man with empty cupboards.

She did laundry, and I phoned about roofing jobs I'd bid

on. She coughed in a back room. I paid bills. Francie went one way, and I went the other. It all felt like slapjack. Bloom sat by the front gate. Sitting on the couch, I heard a little girl say, "Hi, doggie. Doggie doggie doggie." Then the girl barked. Near midnight, Francie stacked five or six boxes against the wall by the front door. She was kind enough to leave her suitcases in the bedroom. I had the set on, HBO, some half-assed documentary about undercover cops. She made coffee and came in and sat next to me. Bloom was hogging the couch, and she scooted him over.

I said, "You found somewhere to go."

She'd telephoned people off and on for a week. She said, "Lily's."

Her sister in Minnesota. I said, "Not what you really wanted."

"Not really."

"Only one who will take you," I said.

Francie said, "Only one."

"And me," I said.

"And you."

I said, "What about your boy? Maybe just for a visit." Me and Francie, we had our histories. Her husband died years before I met her. They'd had the one son. I had an ex who was robbing convenience stores with the lunatic she ran off with. I bailed them out once, then washed my hands of her. Francie's boy drove up here one summer, and the three of us went out to dinner. He was a smart kid putting himself through college. We had sports we could talk about. He played college baseball. Second base. You needed speed for that. Me, I was third baseman, quick but no wheels, lead feet. I had an arm that could gun you out from my knees. Even now, you laced one down the line, and I'd short-hop it, leap, and nail you.

Francie said, "Not a possibility. He's got roommates. Probably women."

"You could write him," I said. "Since he doesn't have a phone."

She said, "Touché."

I'd already told her I'd move out and she could keep the house. Her answer was, *Leaving here is part of it.* By *here* she meant the city. For all its size, it was an ignorant hick town. People saw AIDS as a judgment from God. The widow woman next door claimed that to hear Elvis sing "Hound Dog" was to know what true love is. Her plan was to volunteer to clean up the sorry mess the Colonel had let Graceland fall into. Stupidity was the rule, but it wasn't why Francie was going.

Bloom was belly up, his legs tossed out, and his eyes rolled back in his head. Francie patted his narrow chest and said, "He likes his back." She had a fox face and pointy fox teeth. She stood up, wigwagging a cigarette she hadn't lit, and she was as tall as the ceiling.

We'd lived together five years, two in this house. We fixed it up and asked the owner about buying it.

Pipe dreams now.

"What's to say?" she said. She lit her cigarette and stuck it in her face.

What I was living with was her standing up on a wooden footstool a couple of weeks ago and telling me to step inside her arms. She held me firm and soberly and then leaned back. She saw the walls not me, and she said, "I've got to go, for good," as if that could mean something between two human beings, something other than a fist crammed down your throat, a fist squeezing the shit out of your heart while it beats.

Not that I hadn't seen her grief in the wind. So, I asked *why* more than any idiot would, and I made a mistake. I said, "What you do is you migrate—is that it? You cut and run."

The spite—her word—in what I said ended whatever it was we were supposed to say to each other.

She clammed up. I'd talk, and she'd raise shaky hands, duck her head, and step out the nearest door. You'd think I was using a bullhorn on her.

The HBO flick ended, and Francie drifted off to bed about two. I sat up, flipped channels, slept on and off, then left at six for a roof I couldn't get out of. I had a crew waiting. We shut down about nine-thirty P.M., and I was in the front door and showered by the time the news came on. Francie worked eight to four-thirty. She did the billing for a refrigeration outfit. Me and her boss, we hunted, and I captained a fast-pitch softball team he sponsored. Francie had told them the time was soon when she'd be going. So today, she went in and told them it was her last day, and they were sad but happy because she must be doing what she wanted to do. Everyone chipped in and bought her an address book, and they wrote their names in it. The book had a cloth cover and a scene on the front of the mountains that surround this valley.

Saturday we washed down the walls of the house, and Francie painted the kitchen and the bedroom we'd used. I timed her car. It was a new VW, and I didn't know its electronics, so I couldn't do much. I changed the belts and oil. I put in new hoses up and down, and I got her a tire from a friend at the Texaco down the street. Her spare was one of those hard-rubber doughnuts that get you from where you had your flat to the nearest gas station at fifteen miles an hour. I loaded her boxes into the backseat. She dragged out her suitcases, and I put them in, thinking, It's only Saturday, can't these wait? That night I saw she'd stacked two changes of clothes on the top of the chest of drawers, her Levi's, two t-shirts, socks, and a pair of shorts for driving.

Sunday I got up, and Francie was in the kitchen, pots on the stove, lids and spoons and plates tossed around like the cupboards had coughed them up. Stock for soup heated on one burner and eggs boiled on another one.

I said, "Is it food they say is the way to a man's heart?"

"It's food," she said.

Francie was slicing vegetables. My first job was to pour jello into a mold filled with bananas. I whipped some cream. Bloom went in and out the screen door.

I said, "You want to go for a ride? Just to talk. We've been good at that, at driving and talking."

Her ad for the TV and dryer had come out, and her plan

was to cook and take phone calls. Packing had left her with odd things to sell.

"One hour," I said. "Out to the lake and back."

She said, "If I can get them on the phone, I can talk them into buying things. If I can actually speak to them. One skill I have is I can sell."

"Later?" I said.

"Maybe."

All the food was to tide me over, was that it? To help me out? To bridge my troubled waters? So if she phoned from Minnesota, the temperature thirty below, she could say, "You doing all right?" and I'd say, "I'm getting by." I'd report that my belly was full.

At one, she took a shower and came out twisting her hair up into a ponytail. She hadn't had any calls. I checked the want ads to see if the phone number was right, and it was. She said, "I'll stir the soup, then let's go."

Bloom heard *go*, and he bounced off her hip. He bit the air.

I said to Bloom, "Where's your leash?"

He had no idea. Finding it wasn't one of his tricks. All he could do was yap. I dug around in the throw pillows and found the leash. I teased him with it, and he hit my hip. He'd tagged me. He jumped from a chair to the couch and stood on his head. He yowled.

Francie, idling in the kitchen doorway, said, "What if someone calls?"

Bloom was by the front door, slapping his leash back and forth.

"They'll call back," I said.

"Maybe."

Bloom spit out his leash, and I did up my shoes.

I said, "You back out now, and you'll break your dog's heart."

She said, "I relent."

"You what?"

"Relent. I relent."

"You'll break my heart," I said.

It was my mother who had looked me up and down one day and said, "Problem is, you and your father, the two of you are no great shakes of a man." Was I paying for that now? For upbringing and biology, for this no-pot-to-piss-in thing we say life is?

Francie said, "We'll talk till we're blue in the face. No one on this planet will ever have to talk again after we've talked today."

We swung up Main and drove into the hills where the rich had cut five-story houses and tennis courts into the mountains and then wrote letters to the editor when deer came down in winter and ate the trees and shrubs. I'd put the roofs on most of the places, and I'd told Francie their stories, who had been raised in town and made money, who had come in from out of state. I grew up here. We'd had two murders, both to do with lovers, and the town council argued every year about what to do with the polygamists who lived off in the woods. Now and then they'd turn up in town looking like mental patients on the loose. I was born a block from where me and Francie lived.

Francie asked me to stop at one house she'd never gotten over. It was set back in a bunch of trees, and the windows she could count added up to thirty-six. I didn't know whose it was. She walked over to a hut where a security guard was sitting.

He came out, carrying his hat, leaned into the fence, and said, "Can I help you?" He was dressed like we'd come to an art gallery. He took himself too seriously.

"Tell me who lives here," she said.

He said, "You looking for someone in particular?"

"Just who lives here. Who on God's earth has thirty-six windows in their house?"

"Can't tell you."

"They're famous. Movies? Politics?"

"Maybe you'd better drive on."

Francie said, "I'm leaving tomorrow, and I'll never be back. I'm departing for good. I won't tell a soul. I'm gone. I'm going to Minnesota, for God's sake." Her Levi's were tight and made her legs come to points at her shoes. Three months back, we'd celebrated her fortieth together. *Quietly,* she'd said. *We celebrate it quietly.* I was, she told me, a witness to her decline. She'd grab her thighs and say, *They're getting thick in front of my eyes.* One day I was working on bids, and she came in and said, "Did you hear a rumbling? Like an avalanche?" She tipped her head, cupped one ear, jabbed a be-silent-finger to her lips, then said, "Hear it? My butt just fell."

Was that it—she didn't want a witness? This bird was taking off because she was getting old? because her feathers had gotten dull? because she needed reading glasses?

The guard said, "If you don't leave, I'll have to call the police." His pants were grey, and then a darker grey stripe ran down the outside seam of each leg. He was a joke and didn't know it.

"I won't tell," she said.

He said, "Why don't you just drive on."

She said, "Going to pull your gun?"

He said, "Ma'am."

She got in the car and said, "Ma'am?"

I bucked my old Chevy up one more hill and rode the brake down the other side. I'd had the car twelve years, and it drove like a bathtub, banging along and taking its own way through corners. Bloom was up in the back window, and I could see him in the rearview mirror. He grinned like a friend of mine.

We stopped at a 7-Eleven, and when Francie went in, Bloom hopped up and stood in her seat. I said to him, "She's one for the books."

Bloom had these baboon eyes, and he could outstare you. We'd had him a year. He focused on the door Francie had gone in. I said, "Cheer up, you say?"

He turned toward me and showed me some worry.

I said, "Easy for you to say."

A long yellow Pontiac twice the size of my Chevy pulled in next to us. The driver had a cauliflower ear. Another man sat in the front seat with him, and there were two women in the back, all in their sixties. One of the women got out and, tugging at her clothes all the way to the door, walked into the 7-Eleven. You could see how she'd make up a bed. The driver cocked his head at Bloom, and Bloom answered him, his head making the same angle in the same direction. It was like they were studying each other through a pipe. The man said, "Hello, doggie."

What had five years added up to?

Me and Francie, we were good people. I worked roofs, a job I'd done since I was eighteen. At forty-five I could put in twenty-four hours when we had to beat rain, humping it through the night, ten or twelve of us on one roof, using spotlights and car lights, me doing what had to be done, whether it was carrying hot or shoveling gravel. I drew the line at shingles. No one on my crew did shingles at night. You lost profits and hacked yourself up some. With lights, nine out of ten times you knocked the shingles home straight, but if you got off you'd be back in the morning and turn a one-day job into three days.

The driver of the Pontiac twisted in his seat so he could see the woman in the back and said, "You know where you can put that idea." He'd gotten loud.

Bloom laid his ears flat to his head and barked.

"Right," the man said. He stared out his windshield and wrenched the steering wheel. His cauliflower ear turned pink. He said, "What pisses me off is they keep telling me to go back where I came from. Why? Because I speak my mind. I say, 'You can't get a meal in this state worth eating.' That's God's truth, and you know it. The next thing I hear is some jerk across the room telling me to go back where I came from."

The woman said, "Garth, you're a horse's ass. Admit it, and then we can go have some real fun."

Garth faked banging his head on the steering wheel. He looked sideways at Bloom and said, "Dog, did you hear that?" Bloom stepped back, wary.

Garth got out of his car and tightened his loose belt. His zipper was down about an inch. He hung here short and round and soft as something you'd float in a swimming pool. He walked to the rear of the car, climbed up on the bumper, and started jumping up and down, yelling, "Garth Hill is a horse's ass."

Francie, carrying Cokes and a magazine, came out and stood by our car, one hand touching it like it was a canyon wall she needed to stay in contact with. She almost dropped the Coke. One of her campaigns was she refused the plastic bags stores put things in. She said hello to Bloom and handed me the Cokes. She'd bought *Shape*.

Garth hopped down, and when he saw Francie he almost fell. He stumbled and reached out.

Francie caught him. She was a lot taller than he was.

"People keep telling me I'm a horse's ass," he said. His voice was this soggy pained thing. He said, "I was passing it on."

"If the horseshoe fits," Francie said.

"Yeah."

She'd hooked him. He liked her.

Francie said to Bloom, "Jump in the back." He did, a trick dog jumping through a hoop.

Garth said, "Sorry."

She patted his arm and reached up and did something to his hair. She said, "Nice hair."

He sucked in his belly.

She said, "Forget it. Life's too short," and poked his stomach. The chicken fat on her arm had wobbled when she'd raised it to his head, and she'd felt that—I knew it, and I wanted her to know deep in her heart that it was okay. Bloom stuck his head out the window. She held his face and said to him, "Your hairdo is wonderful. Who is your beautician?" Bloom curled his tail over his back.

Garth opened the car door for Francie and said, "That's a great dog."

"He is," she said and got in. She said, "Thank you."

"We had a dog like that," Garth said.

Francie guided Bloom through the bucket seats and into her lap. She said to him, "Did you hear what that man said about you?"

The woman who had gone into the 7-Eleven had come out and was standing in front of Garth's Pontiac. She said, "We did. He's a poodle, right?" She was hugging two sacks, potato chips poking out of the top of one of them, beer in the other one.

Francie said, "And terrier."

Garth took the beer from the woman, and she said to Francie, "Is it a little boy or a little girl?"

"A little boy," Francie said.

Garth let her into their car, then skipped around to his side, stood by his door, and said, "You take care of that dog. Don't let anything happen to that dog."

"We don't," Francie said.

Thursday, in the park, eating the fried chicken, I'd said to Francie, "Keep the house and stay. You and Bloom. It's yours, and I'll move. You won't know I'm in town."

She'd said, "You, the house—you got it wrong."

Her arm in mine, the two of us walking back to the house, Bloom up ahead sniffing fence corners and stumps, she'd said only one final thing. She'd said, "I don't want this to be acrimonious."

And I'd thought, *Acrimonious?* Where do you buy words like that? Who uses them?

We followed Garth's Pontiac out of the 7-Eleven until they turned south onto a freeway entrance and we headed for the lake.

"Nice people," Francie said.

I said, "Drunk?"

"Maybe. I don't know. He fell and stepped on me."

Bloom's face floated in the rearview mirror.

Francie had a way of wrapping both her hands around a glass when she drank. A lot of people put their hands all the way around cups. You see them. They'll be in a booth, listening or talking, killing time, and both hands are holding a cup of coffee. It's like it's warming them up. I'd say to Francie, *A drink?*, and show her a bottle, usually bourbon, and she'd get a glass and say, *Two fingers*. Then she'd wrap the glass up in both hands and rest its lip on her chin and talk.

Someday someone will hold a glass the way Francie did, and a picture of Francie will fly up and hit me in the face, and I won't be able to stop it.

Things stick.

There's a hair spray I smell in a crowd, and it takes me back to when I was seventeen. I'm with a girl, and it's late afternoon. We're at her house. Her parents are gone. We're listening to records. Me and her, we're playing records, and the TV is on, a black-and-white set. No sound, she's turned it off. Her back's to me, and I'm behind her, shoved into the cushions. Her hair spray is dry. It smells dry. We're talking, and then I wake up, and it's dark. She stands and says, "Let's go out to the lake. There are things you need to know, and one of them is how to do it in a Volkswagen. I'm going to teach you. I'm giving free lessons."

The picture of Francie will hit me in the face, and I don't know what I'll feel or say. What I do know is I will see her, the glass denting her chin, and I'll hear her. She'll be saying, "I don't want this to be acrimonious."

Me and Francie and Bloom, we drove straight into a sun that sat in the sky like it had been told to stay put. Francie angled the rearview mirror so Bloom could see her, and she tapped it. She said, "Bloom, look. Bloom, it's Francie and Bloom." He zeroed in on her, and she said, "Bloom, it's Bloom." She tapped the mirror, and his lip dropped.

Francie punched my arm and said, "He saw us. Did you see that?"

"He saw you?"

"Us. Bloom and Francie."

Bloom coughed.

I said, "Dogs don't see in color, do they?"

"He understands," she said.

I said, "They don't see flat stuff, do they? Pictures, things like that."

From where I sat, I saw only Francie's eyes hanging there in the mirror.

When we'd get close to drunk on a weekend, we'd roll back

the chairs and coffee table and Francie'd get Bloom up on his hind legs. She'd lift his front paws up high, stretch his legs out. She'd sing to him, and he'd sing back. She sang about the muffin girl. Wondered if Bloom had seen her. Her finish was she'd let go of one of Bloom's paws and turn him through a twirl he did like he was a five-year-old. He put one clumsy foot over the other one and acted worried.

The drive to the lake took twenty minutes. Coming in from above the water, we could see the sun had sucked the color out of it. I parked by a tree, and Francie said she'd stay where she was. She said, "I can see what I want from here." Me and Bloom, we ran down to the shore, and he headed for the waves. Bloom got in water at the drop of a hat. On a walk he'd find sprinklers or try to dip in ditches. He loved to soak in water. I pulled my shirt off over my head, sat on a rock, and let its warmth seep into me. I'd had some cancer burned from the top of my head, and the sun picked at the spots. Two women tossed a Frisbee for Bloom, and near the beach the windsurfers kept standing up on their boards and then falling into the water. Out on the lake, some boats skipped along. Waterskiers whipped back and forth behind them. More windsurfers, half a mile out, sailed across the wakes caused by the boats and changed direction quick as thinking. They tacked into the wind and out of it. Their sails were bright and transparent and lit by the sun, and they flashed against the blue hills beyond the lake. I'd never windsurfed, but I'd sailed, and I felt the muscles they were using.

I went to the car for a cap, and Francie said, "Bloom okay?"

"He's made friends," I said. He was running from one woman to the other one. I said, "Come and see."

She said, "He'll shake off in the car."

I found my cap and a towel and laid the towel on the back seat. Bloom barked. One of the women had on a day-glo orange bikini, and the other one wore a classy black one-piece. They were women out of the ads on TV.

I walked back down, and Francie slipped out of the car and sat on the hood, smoking, her pack next to her.

She had two ways of smoking. One was she'd make a V and cram her cigarette down in there. You knew she had something to say when she smoked like that, and you knew she wouldn't hold in for long what was bugging her. She looked like she was biting her hand when she drew on the cigarette. Her other way was to keep the cigarette near the tips of her fingers where it stabbed at things. You knew she was retreating then. She'd pull smoke in, and her face would collapse into the lips she'd made. She was getting deep into unhappiness when she smoked this way.

I rolled up my pants and waded out, and Bloom, all head and feet, splashed toward me. He stopped, floated, enjoying it, not touching the bottom, just being a dog in some water. Me and the women got him into a three-corner game of Frisbee. Bloom leaped up and barked and snagged a toss only when we let him. We tired him out.

I threw up my hands and said, "Ladies, we've got to go."

They made frowns you could see from across the lake, and the one in the bikini knelt down and hugged Bloom in the shallow water. She kissed him right directly on his lips and said, "Stick around?"

The other one said, "We keep the dog if you go."

They thought I was younger than I was. Work had kept me solid. No sloppy fat on me, and I weighed less than I did in high school.

I said, "I got a lady in the car and a pot of soup on the stove."

The one holding Bloom said, "Dog's ours then."

"You want him, you got him," I said. "Save us some trouble."

She said, "You dumping this dog?"

"Not the dog."

She said, "There's a party tonight," and let Bloom down.

The one in black suit said, "We took a vote, and we want you."

"That's appreciated, ladies," I said. I called Bloom, and he ran up to me and shook, his wet legs nothing but skinny black bones. You could snap one by looking at it too long. I said, "Another day."

Bikini said, "That party tonight—follow the noise, and bring the dog and your own beer."

Me and Bloom headed up the path to the car. I dried him off in the parking lot, and the two of us ran a couple of short races. We'd reach a spot, and I'd bend over, and he'd lick at my nose. He'd put a paw up, and I'd take it.

The phone was ringing when we opened the door to the house, and Francie hurried to pick it up. A neighbor was calling about his roof. I put him off, told him I'd come by at the end of the week.

I showed Bloom a bottle of bourbon and said, "Drink?"

The phone rang.

Francie answered it, and me and Bloom, we went into the kitchen and had a peek at the soup. We tasted it, first me, then him. It was done. I could hear Francie. She was saying, "It's a bargain. You can steal them. Buy the TV and the dryer, buy both, and I'll give you a third off. I'll throw in juice glasses and a spice rack."

I ladled soup into two bowls and carried one into Francie. I said, "Mention Bloom." She took the soup, and I got mine and some spoons. I gave Bloom a full bowl.

She was telling someone called Rose how to get to the house.

I said, "Maybe Rose can use a dog."

Francie turned away from me.

"Rose and Bloom," I said. "It's fate. Like the landscapers, Moss and Grassly. Like Cutter, who sells lawn mowers."

She placed her soup on a bookcase and pulled the cord and herself around the hallway corner.

I set my soup next to Francie's and went after her. I circled by and got in the way. I put my hands around my mouth and pretended to shout, but whispered, "Bloom."

Francie wouldn't square up to me. She gave me a shoulder, then a hip. She knocked into to me getting out of the hallway. She said into the phone, "I'll hold them. But hurry, though. I've been taking calls all day."

I said, "Liar."

She hung up and came at me like I was a drunk who had rear ended her car. I thought she'd cracked the phone hanging it up. She said, "Don't bash at me. Don't bash at me when I'm on the phone, when I'm talking to someone."

"Bash at you?"

"Yes."

I raised my hands, saying, "No problem."

She said, "If I'm somewhere, you're there. You're within a foot of me, even if it's just in my head. Talking. Something. Bashing at me. Wherever I am, there you are. It's like I'm being followed by a boulder, a big rock. You know those signs, Warning Falling Rocks—the way you feel when you see one of those signs on a mountain road."

She went down the hall, and I heard a door shut.

I said to Bloom, "Bash at her? Falling rocks? Warning, falling rocks? A boulder?"

Five years ago we'd met, and we'd talked and liked each other. I'd eaten with her boy. Me and him, we'd played golf a few times.

Francie and me, we'd put together thousands of words. Who keeps records? One day you say five hundred words, then maybe twenty the next day. Maybe on a Saturday you say a thousand words. Who knows?

Today we hadn't said six words that counted.

The phone rang, and I told some sad voice that there was a washer with the dryer. I said, "Hurry. It's a bargain. Someone will beat you to it."

The voice said, "And the TV, too?"

"And the TV," I said.

I sat on the couch, and then Francie was behind me, saying, "I'll take Bloom."

Bloom hopped up and spread out next to me, on his back, his legs poked out and his weary head full of sleep.

I said, "Tuckered out, boy?"

I thought I'd learned what I was put here on earth to learn, but if I had, I'd have understood I could live to be ninety and someone would come down the pike and pull the rug out from under me. Out of left field, I'd be sucker punched.

Francie said, "Remember that dog show, the big one on cable. The Maltese won best in show. They said, 'Maltese talk only to poodles, and poodles talk only to God.'"

I said, "Day after day, me and you, we're doing things. What does it add up to? All we've said and done, does it add up to something? To good company—is that it? It adds up to good company."

She came around and sat across from me.

I said, "We need something you uncork. Wine. Champagne. Did you pack the corkscrew? Where's the crystal? The silver and the china?"

Francie got up and moved Bloom over. She sat by me, and her knee touched mine.

I said, "We didn't talk."

She fit her hands to her face, then opened them, peek-a-boo, the way you kid a baby, and said, "Nothing sad, once you look at it."

I got up on the couch, and I jumped from cushion to cushion. Bloom flew off. I cupped my hands around my mouth and yelled, "I'm a horse's ass. I'm a horse's ass."

Francie knelt down, and Bloom came over. Somehow he stood for the hole we'd dug for ourselves. She said, "I was wrong. That's sad, real sad."

I said, "I'm amazed," and I sat down.

She said through her hands, "Don't be."

But I was, and I am, and I will be.

I'm a forty-five-year-old roofer, and I sat there amazed. What did you expect?

Lake Stink

Like pitching a baseball, you don't aim a handshake. Uncle Ajax teaches me this. He has me handshake until I get it right. He also tells me you don't go poking your hand at a lady unless she offers hers first. We're on the putting green at the Tropicana Country Club, Las Vegas, Nevada, and I'm seventeen. Uncle Ajax's really A. J. Jackson. He and I are taking on two of his casino buddies, best ball, thirty-six holes, and he wants me to be clearheaded brainy kin he can be proud of. No greenhorns allowed. He gave me the Bull's Eye putter I'm using.

I will be thirty-one, married, living just north of Salt Lake City, Utah, when I learn that Uncle Ajax is not my uncle. Annie, my mother, flies American West out of Vegas, loses an hour to one time zone, rents a car, and drives passionately the oddly circular roads to our place. For a month, day after day, my father Roland has accused her of having an affair with Uncle Ajax. He's ragged Annie to death. His evidence involves a vacation to Mexico, four A.M., sand in her swimsuit, and a missing thong.

In our kitchen, she rips drawers open and bangs them shut, slaps Formica and walks in circles. She won't sit down. Her lips don't line up, and her eyes jiggle. Her hair's dipped itself into the shape of a bucket seat. All she can do is mutter corny sentiments. She says, "Love is unconditional," and "Love is never being sorry, ever."

Gina, my wife, says, "A fling with Uncle Ajax?"

Uncle Ajax stops over with me and Gina now and then.

Uses our guest room, dries himself with our towels. He mails us golf tees with our names engraved on them in gold. He has this greying art-deco face, and he dresses in fruit colors. Hair as white, thick, swirly as whipped cream, and trained. He wears Pat Boone shoes.

Annie picks up Gina's hand, squeezes it kindly, and says to me, "He's not your uncle. It was a way we had of talking back then."

She and Gina sit down at the kitchen table, Gina saying, "A Dutch uncle?"

"That's a different thing," Annie says, and she twirls the lazy Susan.

I say, "Did you, with him?"

Annie says, "Don't go highhatting me."

"Highhatting you?" I say.

She says, "I'm not yours to scold." She's stacking up wheat thins and softly crying.

Five times she comes, and we put her up. Roland phones, writes, telegraphs, drives to Salt Lake, leaves notes, sends flowers, buys pewter, sterling silver, diamonds. He hunts down antique Valentines and has them delivered. Frilly messages, fat cupids pointing tin arrows, blood red hearts beating at the end of short wobbly springs. One says, "Roses are red, violets are blue. Without your morning song, everything's wrong." She repacks, kisses my cheek and Gina's, and rides off with him. The sixth time she refuses Roland's calls and gifts and disappears when he shows up. He trots from bush to bush across our grass. He hires three fiddlers and stands out front, his pants rolled up to his knees, his moon face on her empty room, and sings, "Three Coins in a Fountain." Their song. We think she's gone to the Hilton out by the airport. We'll learn after he leaves she's at Henriquet's, next door, where she saw it all. After a month, Roland goes home.

Next day, Annie moves in with us. Gina introduces her to the ugly pleasure of cigars, and the two of them fill our wastebaskets with the ashes of Roland's letters and telegrams. The last one said, *All is forgiven [stop]*.

Lake Stink

Annie kept us as homebase and flew off to visit her friends and her other children, my brothers and sisters. By accident, she bumped into Uncle Ajax in Pullman, Washington. They ate crab, hit a movie, and he put his arm in hers and came back here when she did.

Uncle Ajax and me, we got to the third hole the day he taught me about handshakes, and I repaid him. He'd caught his six iron fat and left it tangled in the snarly grass short and right of the stick. He pulled out his seven and put it back, his nine, his wedge, then scratched his ass. I clasped his shoulder and said, "Your wedge, and deadhand the shot. The ball'll come out gentle as an egg." I buried one of my own Titleists in the nasty rough, stepped on it, and then dropped a deadhanded wedge on top of it. The ball popped up, caught, rolled, and found the cup. On seventeen, after Uncle Ajax had lost control of his approach on sixteen, I taught him the knockdown shot he hit into a thirty-mile-an-hour crosswind that had come up. He birdied the hole.

Back then, Ajax'd call Roland and say he was coming to town. That night or the next morning, he'd jerk his yacht-sized Olds 88 into our driveway, tip me to carry in his luggage and golf bag, try to rough up my hair, hug Annie loosely, and handshake Roland. He slept in my room. There were two beds, one against the south wall and under a painting of a Bengal tiger, and one against the north wall and under a painting of a panther. The frames were fake bamboo. My bed was under the panther. It was Uncle Ajax who told me panthers trick you into the jungle by crying like a human baby. He sat on the other side of the room from me, humped up on the bed in his underwear, and said, "Everyone needs someone in their life who'll lie to them."

French doors in my room opened out onto the backyard. The sun came up early, and lying in my bed I'd see this white thing lying on the throw rug by Uncle Ajax's shoes. It belonged on a woman, had buckles and straps, looked stretchy. Annie told me it was a corset. "His back," Annie said. "Uncle Ajax has a bad back."

Over breakfasts, Ajax shaving down the hall, she'd bitch to Roland. "The man comes here on less than a minute's notice," she said. "I boil him eggs how he likes them. I make his bed, I hunt up his socks, I wash his clothes. He goes down to the business, takes out a slug of money, and drives off scot-free and in cold blood. You better watch out. He's a loafer." When Ajax came in and sat at the table, his monumental hair perfect, his face pink, she snapped their food onto their plates and refused to sit. She stood off by the refrigerator dipping toast in egg yolk, her cup of coffee at her elbow, her eyes cleat holes in her face.

That night, Roland and Annie snug in bed, Roland would say, "It's as much his as it's ours."

It was their business together, air conditioning and sheet metal.

Uncle Ajax spent his days selling and playing golf, and he took me along. His corset choked off his swing. He yanked clubs back like he was tugging at something and then lashed at the ball, and he chilly-dipped his short irons. Still, he hit the fairways and got enough distance. He played to an eleven handicap. He walked like a man in wooden shoes but putted lights out.

That history lies behind us here on mine and Gina's back patio. The lawn dips and flows and heaves itself over a third of an acre before it slopes toward the Great Salt Lake, which is a couple of miles to the west.

It's evening. Gina is upstairs helping Annie get ready for a date with Uncle Ajax. Me and Ajax, we sip Dewar's and stroll to the edge of the yard. I lug our bottle along. We played Park Meadows today. Age and his stiffening back have reduced Uncle Ajax's game to what amounts to a tree hoping it can swing the clubs and not die doing it. He's got no backswing, just sort of punches and swipes at the ball. He's had his neck vertebrae fused.

I've cut an elevated tee into the grass, and we sit on it. The sun's a big brassy doorknob out there over the lake.

Lake Stink

Next door, Henriquet tosses feed to his chickens. He says, "*Amis, amis. L'amour, la folie,*" and they kick twigs, gulp down pebbles, and cluck back at him. His one rooster, a disgruntled wheat yellow no-bigger-that-a-fist black-winged bantam, broods on the coup.

The lake smells bad. We've walked into a rotten egg out here. It's lake stink, the bad marriage of salt brine and high humidity. It's soured our drinks.

"Not a real attraction, is it?" Ajax says. He holds his nose.

I dump my Dewar's, and he dumps his.

The smell's so bad it hurts.

I refill his drink and mine and say, "Let's see if we can kill it."

Henriquet told me Roland is living in a sheep camp out near Tooele, Utah. Annie has an injunction against his being within a certain radius, but wherever she is there are rumors he's nearby. She visits my sister in Ely, Nevada, and hears Roland got a room in McGill up the road. She stops for a week in St. George, Utah, and the word is he's fishing the Virgin River out by Hurricane. She says the feeling is the one you get when you hear news reports about some killer walking away from a work detail at the state prison.

Behind me and Ajax the sliding glass door smacks open, and Annie and Gina walk out onto the patio arm-in-arm. They look like prom night. Ajax slogs down his drink, rolls himself off the lawn, and starts a wounded-duck jog toward them, saying, "Oh my oh."

Mother looks good. She had Gina cut her hair, and it's smart. It's classy, soft as cloth and young. Her dress flutters.

Ajax tosses his tumbler over his shoulder.

Annie shuts her eyes, seems to flinch, then opens them, and they glisten.

Lake stink, it'll tear anyone up.

Ajax's tumbler thuds in the grass, and he has picked up speed, is making fresh long keep-on-trucking strides that deny even a hint of hip, back, or leg trouble. He is saying, "We'll paint the town red," and reaching for Annie, his palms open.

Next morning, I'm in the kitchen at six-thirty, and if I didn't know better I'd say the lake was pretty. Its colors roam from periwinkle blue to a lead grey to an avocado green to teal. I'm hung like a dope over the coffee machine. I've got the windows open. On the cupboard, Ajax has taped maps of Wyoming and Utah and written across the bottom *FIND YOURSELF IN WYOMING.* He cut the corner off Utah and trimmed Wyoming so they match up, and he's traced three routes out of Salt Lake into Yellowstone. A stretch of I-80 from Sage to Kemmerer is circled. Ajax was born in Big Piney, Wyoming, and he and Annie are planning a trip up around Bear Lake in Utah, then on into Kemmerer and a stop in Big Piney before they head for Grand Teton and Yellowstone.

Gina and Annie pass behind me, and I say, "Coffee?"

Annie says to Gina, "But my earlobes crack." She rubs and tugs at her left one.

"Hand cream," Gina says.

I'll check in later to see if I exist.

Outside, Henriquet lopes through our backyard, a white hen the size of a child under his arm, six or seven more hot-footing toward his place. Henriquet jogs like the hens, like circus clowns in big feet. I'd help, but he's proud. He's had the hens clipped and still they escape.

Henriquet, low to the ground, under fire, zips left, then right. Dust flies. The hens are bumper cars. They hit each other, wobble off, cluck and clack. They're brainless creatures. Henriquet, in neon pink shorts and a v-neck t-shirt, is reminding me of the dads of the kids I grew up with in Vegas.

I take coffee to Annie and Gina at the kitchen table. I say, "Hard to get into the cupboards," and point at Ajax's maps.

They're talking fingernails, Annie saying, "I paid forty for these, and I've got ridges." She shows Gina.

Gina picks at one of the nails.

Annie says, "I tried silk wraps."

"You could end up with fungus," Gina says.

"Underneath?"

"And you could lose them. My sister, hers fell off."

Lake Stink

Annie taps her nails on the table.

Gina says, "Those'd give me claustrophobia."

Annie studies her nails. They're long and curly.

A hen flings itself at Henriquet's face, and he stumbles backwards, throws out an arm, and drops the one hen he caught. He spits and stamps at them. They're not afraid. They'll kick his butt. Another one flies at his hip, all spurs and tail feathers.

Out front, Ajax honks and comes booming through the door. He waves more maps and the Wyoming Vacation Guide at us, saying, "Find yourself in Wyoming." He's got postcards. He spreads them out and says, "Let me tell you something beautiful. Sun isn't up yet, and there's this rose color on everything. You and me, Annie, we're the only ones up at the lodge. We make that noise people make when they walk across a wooden porch. We can see all the way to Elk Island. Your arm's around me, and we're a little off balance. Jackson Lake is black and silver, so smooth you know we could walk across it."

Henriquet sees me in the window and nods. He raises his arms, saying *What's a guy to do?* The hens have scattered.

Ajax is talking about big horn sheep and air so crisp it rustles when you walk through it. He says, "Let me tell you about the Green River. Moose. Black bear. Snow King Mountain. Cutthroat trout."

By the time I wash my cup, unlock the sliding glass door, and head out to help, Henriquet's on his side of the short cinder block fence. He's bribing the hens with bits of Butterfinger. This works. He sees me and says, "Hang on. Just a minute." The hens follow him into their coop.

The sun's come full up. It'll heat the lake, and the stink will thicken.

Henriquet heads for a tool shed, saying, "Got something for you to see. Stick around."

I wander out to my practice tee. From here, most evenings, I drive old golf balls at the lake. Gina's bought me a metal driver I haven't tried yet. I've held out, stuck with wood.

"Hey," Henriquet says. He sets one of his bird sculptures

on top of the fence. It's a turkey vulture. "Heft it," he says. "Roland commissioned me."

I look it in the eye.

Henriquet bolts and welds into bird sculptures old tools, rake tines, used car parts, springless springs. He sets the birds up so they stand guard over the holes of the miniature golf course that fills up two-thirds of his backyard. It's the only natural grass one I've ever seen. He mows it every morning just before the sun rises. He still needs to make birds for seventeen and eighteen. Henriquet's done one roadrunner. It's at least three-feet tall, has a tractor seat body, pitchfork prongs for tail feathers painted red, white, and blue, tire-iron legs, a bicycle sprocket for its head, and an orange light bulb for its beak. There are grouse, pheasant, and quail, and there is one crane, its body a plow blade. The turkey vulture is hatchbacked like Dracula. Its head is a claw hammer painted black and red and welded upside down onto a wrought-iron neck. The wings are a shovel blade, Dracula's cape. Henriquet used a spent howitzer shell for the body and spray-painted it orange. The shoulders are two disks he salvaged from a car clutch. The vulture has perfect balance when I put it back down. I say, "You talked to Roland?"

"He comes by. I go see him."

"When?"

"At night, early morning."

We sit on the fence, and Henriquet lights a cigarette. He smokes because he watches old movies on AMC. He's from an island just off Cuba. Castro, he's told me, sent AIDS to the U.S. Henriquet's leaving his island had something to do with his printing shop.

Out of the back of his house, swinging down from a balcony, is the kind of stairway you see in Hollywood musicals, the one the starlet descends, her sequined gown twinkling, men waiting at the bottom of the steps ready to pick her up and carry her to center stage. It's the reason Henriquet bought the place. He's painted the stucco house pink.

Henriquet says, "Want to deliver this with me?"

"Sure," I say. "When?"

"Later. About two." He picks up the vulture and says to me, "Come. Try out my new hole."

We end up near the stairs. He hands me a putter and says, "Give it a shot."

The new hole zigs and zags, then humps up, and swings left. There's a forest of six-inch plastic pine trees at the top of the hump and a trail through them. The bird that hovers over this hole is a woodpecker. I bow to the bird to show my respect. Then I clap. I'm asking for its attention and its help. This pleases Henriquet. He drops a ball for me, and I line it up. My putt doesn't even make the hump. Henriquet puts his foot on the retaining wall that borders the course, his toe marking the hole-in-one-spot, the place where a bank shot will send the ball through the zig and zag, up the hill, past the trees, and into the cup. He says, "Medium speed. Say a twenty-footer, slightly uphill on that bent-grass crap you grew up on in Vegas."

I bow to the woodpecker, then clap. I hit the spot, but my speed's off, and the ball makes the hump only to slip by the hole on the left. I nail the next one. The ball zigs and zags, slides up the hump, weaves through the trees, and drops dead center.

"Genius," I say to Henriquet.

He says, "Praise be to the gods."

Back at the fence, he stubs out a cigarette, pockets the butt, and says, "I'll honk for you at two."

I hop the fence.

He says, "Roland comes by at three, or four, every morning. I shut off the TV and light up the course. He shows no respect to the gods, to the birds. Offers them nothing, no homage. Won't clap. Won't bow. And he takes me for nickels and dimes, hole-in-one after hole-in-one."

"Every night."

"Almost."

"I need to see him," I say.

"Annie stands up there," Henriquet says, and he points at the alcove at the top of the stairs in our house. There's a big arched window. "Your house is dark, but I can see her. She smokes and crosses her arms over her chest. Roland don't seem to see her. Don't act like he does. But you can bet your last dollar, he does. He's playing for her. She might be naked. It's hard to tell."

I look up at the window. I had no idea.

Henriquet says, "*Coup de foudre.*"

Henriquet's stiff buckshot pick-up throws us off I-215 and into Tooele, Utah. The road's thin and knocks us around. The white line separating the lanes disappeared years ago. Wheat grass grows five-feet high in ditches that run along the sides, and it's dry. You can hear this place crackle. A fire'd wipe the town out. The houses stand three-feet apart, cracker boxes, clapboard siding. Chicken wire fences around the yards. No screens. No doors. No sidewalks. You can imagine the fly problem.

We find Main Street, which amounts to a pool hall, its windows boarded up, three bars dirt ugly and sealed shut, broken neon, and a tire shop. We head west. You know that in some U-shaped shoe-box-sized adobe motel a local high school football player whose IQ is seventy on a good day, whose one dream and only hope is a job at Kennecott's copper mine after graduation, is holed up in the room farthest from the street and is abusing his high school sweetheart in ways only his pea-brain can dream of.

Along a dirt lane, behind a lime-green house, we locate Roland. He's sitting under a patio umbrella. It's orange and has white loopy trim, says TAMPA on it. There's a round patio table in front of him. His chair rests him against his sheep camp. He lets it ride forward and toss him at us. He snags two beers from a cooler. He's grown a goatee, and I'd say he's lost fifty pounds. He looks like celery.

I've seen this movie before.

Henriquet juggles the vulture he's wrapped in a blanket and grabs his beer. I wave mine off.

"Suit yourself," Roland says.

Lake Stink

I say, "Fat," and show him my belly.

Something about Roland says he's become a grim s.o.b.

The sheep camp's like a gypsy wagon slapped to the flatbed of an old truck. The sides are wooden, painted forest green, and the top is curved corrugated sheet metal. It's got a back door you'd see on a fancy house and a screen door. You have to climb a step ladder to get in. The truck is one of those prehistoric GMCs put together in the fifties. It's faded red, has a white grill in front thick as a cattle guard on a train, headlights like animal eyes, five basic moving parts under the hood, and a cab a boulder couldn't dent.

Outside, under a lean-to, are a washer and a dryer, both running. There's a motorcycle up on blocks and hooked to a generator by a regular pants belt.

Roland's got a TV on, NASCAR. The set's banked up against a rock in the shade of the umbrella. He used to drive stock, or maybe it was he raced bikes on ice up in Canada. There's a cordless phone lying by his chair.

He holds the vulture like it's a baby.

"What do you think?" Henriquet says.

Roland stands the bird on the ground and circles it. He squats next to it and strokes its wings. He tugs, twists, and scratches his goatee.

Henriquet sucks on his beer.

The phone rings, and Roland sidearms a rock at it. He shakes out a handkerchief and wipes the bird off.

In a field next to his sheep camp, mules and sheep and ducks huddle under a cottonwood tree. The sheep look sad. The mules, sleek, strong, athletic wide-faced animals, form spokes around the trunk of the tree, their heads pressed into it. They say you can train them to guard sheep. A creek runs past the animals.

Roland says, "It's a work of art."

"No shit," Henriquet says.

"No shit." Roland invites us to sit, and he takes his chair. I land on the cooler, and Henriquet finds a box.

I say, "Your sheep?"

"No, Sir," Roland says.

I *have* seen this movie.

The washer stops, and the phone rings again. Roland kicks at it. It keeps ringing. "No one on it," he says. "Thing's no good. Rings for no good reason. Or it'll be one of them recordings."

Them? This man has ten or twelve years of college in him.

On TV, we're getting a shot from inside one of the cars. Driver's bumper-to-tail with the car in front of him. There's some break up on the screen, but you get the feel of it. They cut to an overhead shot.

Roland says to Henriquet, "What say we do it?"

"Ready when you are."

They're going to weld the vulture to Roland's truck, turn it into a hood ornament. Got to be illegal. No way can you see around it. Henriquet's brought the torch, oxygen, everything they need.

I say, "Coke?"

"Inside," Roland says, and he snaps welding goggles over his face.

His refrigerator's our old Maytag, but it seems shorter than it was in the house. Annie wanted nothing but Maytag. Roland's got a slot machine in here, a stove, a brass bed, and several thousand paperback westerns. My photograph's here. My sisters'. And Annie's. I see two pistols, six-shooters. They're the ones you see in magazines, advertised as the real McCoys.

Back outside, sitting in Roland's chair, under his umbrella, I sip Coke and watch the races. Behind me is the snap and pop of their welding, and on the screen the cars suck past a camera that's right down there on the track.

Would I have recognized Roland on the street?

I don't think so.

He's wearing cowboy boots, deep-dyed green and red geometric designs curling up the sides, loops for pulling the boot on. If he panhandled me on a downtown street, I'd give him a buck and walk on by.

The mules seem stuck to the tree. The sheep look sadder.

Roland was a CPA, had a MBA from Berkeley, and a law degree from Duke. Where'd that guy go to? the one who spoke Latin?

The cars zing by on the screen.

Henriquet finishes his welding, lifts up his goggles, and says, *"Fini."*

"Work of art," Roland says.

They touch beers.

The vulture is magnificent.

Henriquet cuts off the torch flame, and Roland jumps up on the bumper. He spits on a spot and buffs the bird's wings. He steps down and backs off, checks the bird out from the front, both sides, and every other possible angle. "Avian perfection," he says to Henriquet.

"Praise be to the gods," Henriquet says.

I say, "Can you see around it to drive?"

"Ain't the point?" Roland says.

I'm telling you he was a CPA.

Henriquet flutters a loose hand at his brow and says, *"Il est bête."*

It's the last roundup. That's the movie. The old gang is getting together to right one last wrong. Eventually they'll ride out and gather up the others, the guy who learned how to tie knots only ancient Chinese men have mastered, the big slow-witted strong-arm mug, and the drunk who'll sober up at the right moment.

We load up Henriquet's gear, and I'm sitting in the truck when Roland says to me, "You tell Annie I said to say hello. Tell her I'm standing fast."

I tell him he'll have to do that.

He says, "I have evidence, you know."

"I understand you do," I say.

"Irrefutable," he says, and I see the old CPA in him. He shifts his feet noiselessly and says, "Not that it matters."

I say, "It's between you two."

"I'm clean," he says. "Innocent, from head to toe."

I raise a hand that says *I bet you are.*

He says, "I see her up there. She watches me at Henriquet's. She smoking?"

"Cigars."

"Real cigars?"

"Real enough."

Henriquet piles in and starts the truck. I say to Roland, "See you around."

He steps back, squints, and says, "Exactly."

Saturday morning, and I'm on my practice tee hitting the new driver Gina got for me. I don't know about metal woods. The sound's off. Did you know the blind golf? They have tournaments and shoot decent scores. But not the deaf. They say you've got to hear the shots. This metal wood is zip, pink. Zip, pink. Zip, pink. I'm getting more distance. No question. My balls end up twenty and thirty yards beyond the cottonwoods I usually aim at. Still, it's like having the refrigerator you bought delivered, and you keep touching it, not sure they brought the one you paid for. Give me a hand-dipped persimmon driver anytime. The balls seem to corkscrew off this metal thing.

Back in the house, Ajax is talking, is telling Gina and Annie beautiful things about Wyoming. How many times can you stand to hear that Wyoming is the rooftop of America? I've had my fill. The RV Ajax rented for their trip fills up our driveway. It's got three bedrooms, two bathrooms, a kitchen, a TV room, a bar, and a quadraphonic CD.

Annie's packed and loaded. She keeps saying to Gina, "Won't you come? We'll have fun." She and Gina are getting food ready.

Ajax's invited Gina and me, but he doesn't mean it.

I hit a drive, and it corkscrews on me, slides right.

Ajax has come up behind me. "I'm in the way," he says. "They sent me out here." He points toward the lake, toward the shot I just hit. "Not your usual stuff," Ajax says.

I tee one up. Zip pink. Another slider. No sweet spot on this thing.

Henriquet has come floating down the back stairs of his house. He's holding up a couple of putters, saying, "Ajax. Ajax."

Ajax wanders toward him.

Annie, probably after something in her bedroom, stands in the window upstairs. Her arms are crossed, and cigar smoke swirls around her.

"One round for a hundred bucks?" Henriquet says.

"For pleasure only," Ajax says. He pokes his hand out to shake, and Henriquet slaps at it.

"*Tu t'es flatté,*" Henriquet says.

Ajax says, "Touché."

Annie brushes hair away from her face, swipes at the cigar smoke. I turn back to my tee. Behind me, Henriquet claps. The bird that stands over the first hole is a whooping crane.

I swing. Zip, pink. Zip, pink. Nothing. I can't hit this club.

I'm bent over teeing up, and I see trouble at Henriquet's. Ajax is putting, and Henriquet is coming at him with a putter raised above his head. Ajax sees him. He's smart. He doesn't duck or step back. He steps into Henriquet, like he's going to hug him. And he does. He's hugging Henriquet when the putter comes down, and it whacks him, but has no force. It twanks and catches between them.

I'm there before they separate, and all I can say is, "What is this?"

Henriquet says to Ajax, "*Éspèce de cretin.*"

"I come here, arms raised, showing you I have no weapons," Ajax says. "Barefoot. I take off my shoes in this your holy place."

Not quite. He's in socks. But his white bucks *are* sitting on top of the fence.

Henriquet slaps at his own wrist, hand under, flat out, says, "*Vas t'en.*"

Annie stands in the window stone cold still. Her arms crossed.

There's a gash on Ajax's forehead.

Last thing Henriquet says to Ajax is, "This is between us,"

and he jabs his putter at Ajax. Ajax sticks his hand out and says, "No hard feelings." Henriquet spits at it and says, "May the hens pluck your eyes out." He sails up the back stairs to his house.

I put an arm around Ajax and help him get into his shoes. We're about to the patio when Henriquet yells from his balcony. He says, "Find yourself in Wyoming," and he aims the putter like it's a rifle. He says, "Cabammm."

Annie's in the kitchen, and she's got the medical kit out. She's lit a fresh cigar.

I say, "Maybe he needs the hospital."

"I don't," Ajax says.

We clean him up and slap on some bandages. He looks like a small boy. He turns to Annie, flashes his snowy teeth, and says, "Find yourself in Wyoming."

"What was that all about?" she says.

Ajax says, "Roland."

She says, "How?"

Gina and I walk out onto the patio. The sun's getting up in the sky, and the lake stink is edging in. We walk out to my tee. I pick up the driver I let drop. She says, "Does it work?"

"It will," I say.

I hit one. Zip, pink.

She says, "Sounds funny."

Some of Henriquet's hens are stomping around on top of the fence, and he's sitting on the stairs that fall into his backyard. His head droops.

Gina says, "Will there be trouble?"

I say, "Could be."

Later, I'm on my tee, working on getting my hands out of my swing, and I catch a drive dead center. I smack it deep and straight. It sounds good. Not the thwack of persimmon, but not the pink I've been getting. More of a zip, ping.

I nail one, and it's then that it hits me, comes over me like a storm over the lake, hits me in big-time drive-in-movie cinematic vision. Ajax and Annie are on their way to Wyoming.

Lake Stink

They're driving up to Bear Lake and then swinging south of it across state road 30 and into Sage, Wyoming. They won't make it. They're traveling on a two-lane paved road, but there's a mountain range they've got to cross. At the top, on a huge boulder, someone's painted in blood red THE TOP. Roland's up there, his sheep camp backed up into one of the fire roads, the rear bumper snug against those gates they lock against sightseers. You can't see him from the highway.

The lake stink is up, is enough to gag me.

I smack a drive toward the cottonwoods. Henriquet, up on his balcony, claps. His hens have stopped jitterbugging around, and they're watching.

If I drove out to Tooele, the sheep camp would be gone. Maybe that phone would be left, that cordless phone would be lying in the weeds. I'd walk over to the fence, and a grey mule would come up to me, and I'd feel its face, suck in its smartness. There's every possibility in the world it might speak to me.

Roland's parked up there on that stretch of highway Ajax circled on the map. Ajax was worried about the summit, about how quickly bad weather can roll in.

The road is narrow. The turkey vulture glints in the dying rays of the sun.

Roland sits in the cab of his prehistoric Ford, drinking Coors and looking hard around the bird. Maybe he didn't toss the phone. Maybe it's lying next to him on the seat, and it's ringing. Henriquet's calling. "They're coming," he says, and he tells Roland the exact time they left.

Roland's six-shooters lie crossed on the dashboard like the picture in the ad I saw. He's wearing a black bandanna and a straw hat that funnels to a droopy point over his brow. His goatee twitches on its own. He squints, chews his lip.

I think deep and swack a drive with the power and velocity of those NASCARs blowing through a straightaway. The ball catches air and drops toward the cottonwoods fifty yards past anything I've hit before. I've knocked it into the heart of the lake stink.

It's then the feeling swoops down on me.

What Roland will do, I don't know. What he's capable of in his new duds is beyond me. But what I do understand now is that he won't let Annie find herself in Wyoming, and I'm filled with admiration and respect and—well, there's no other word for it—love for the old guy.

L'amour.

I hit a drive thirty yards past the one I just hit.

Behind me, Henriquet claps, and I hear the feathers of all his birds flap and rustle. Or maybe it's angel wings.

Roland's got my attention.

L'amour, la folie.

Our Secret's Out

God, how the plucky bug Lola. The blind at their pianos. Artists who have no hands but stick pencils in their teeth and draw. All the cripples scrambling up mountain sides. The armless Hispanic playing the guitar with his toes, singing hymns for the Pope. And Charles Rook, the man she calls Chuck Lightfoot, his wife Abby, his peppy son and newborn baby girl, his working weekends and nights and his going to med school days, his wheelchair full of those legs dumb as rags.

Earlier, the sky the grey it is before the sun gets up over the mountains, Lola stood on the top landing of the iron stairway that climbs the outside of the house to Walt's attic apartment, and she saw Charles roll down the wooden ramp he's built and wheel himself across the grass and down the driveway into the street. He had on flashy runner's tights and an orange t-shirt that named a 10-K he'd finished. He wears his left shoe on his right foot and his right shoe on his left foot, and they float on the wheelchair like wrong-headed boats. He was headed out on what he calls his morning run, what Lola calls the unfortunate burden of his hope. He'll put in ten or fifteen miles.

Morning after morning, she stands here and thinks, Give up, for God's sake. Please. She says softly, "Chuck Lightfoot." She wants to pitch rocks at him.

Now it is seven A.M., and Lola's bone weary. She'd kill for sleep. Half an hour ago Walt got out of bed and began pacing like troubled thought itself. He took the quilt, left her under one sheet, and it's not doing the job. She's cold. It's his daybed and his apartment, the attic in one of three houses he owns. His dad left him money, and Walt's used it well. Lola's legs ache. She sleeps in socks, and one's strangling her foot.

Walt stops at the breakfast counter, claps, spins around, and comes back eating a handful of vitamins he's poured from a Mason jar. He's megadosing B-complex and vitamin C. The quilt covers him like a piece of blue sky. He says, "To be heard is first."

All the windows are open, and Lola can't get warm. It's fall. She rolls up her unruly sock.

"Understanding is later," Walt says. "Understanding is second."

Last night was the third night he played Toad in *Toad of Toad Hall* at the Pierpoint Street Theater, and he's angry. If you asked, he'd agree that all productions have problems. Maybe it's the script or the lighting, and floorboards can't be trusted. Once it was flimsy scenery, a drop set that wobbled in like a sea gull. Some nights it found its slot. Most nights it didn't. The trouble with *Toad of Toad Hall* is acoustics. Walt swears when he's on stage it's like he's talking into a pillow. He claims he can't be heard.

"Here," Walt says, "I'll show you. I'll illustrate. You'll see." He carries a chair to the middle of the room, centers it on a throw rug, goes to the door, and picks up a coat rack. He twirls it over his head like some gloomy ape in a zoo, then sets it next to the chair. The entrance to act 2 has gone wrong, has left him mumbling into a curtain, and he is blocking it out for Lola. Her understanding what has gone wrong is life and death to Walt. He says, "You have to be heard. To be heard is number one. Understanding? If it comes, it comes."

Lola wishes she had her contacts in. Everything is fuzzy, and she's edgy. Who knows, she could be ambushed. Her leg jerks, and she fights plugging her ears. What's coming she's heard before.

"This is theater," Walt says. He sits by Lola. "And theater, after all, is theater."

She says, "Touch me and I'll break your wrist." Right now

one of his you're-a-good-girl pats would send her weeping into the city. She'd sprint barefooted and goofy into the nasty rush-hour traffic.

Walt gets up, and she grabs for the quilt and misses. He skips away, saying, "What if we did this?" He moves the coat rack to the other side of the chair, tips it at her as if it's taking a bow, and says, "Suppose this is Ratty."

Ratty is Water Rat. In *Toad of Toad Hall*, Ratty is clever and serious, and Toad is slow and foolish. It is Ratty who leads Toad and the other River Bankers when they retake Toad Hall from the Wild Wooders.

A bus stops outside. If Lola could get hold of a hammer, she'd nail the windows shut. She's freezing. She sits against the headboard and hugs her knees.

"Here," Walt says. He's come back over. He says, "Lie down."

"I'm cold." Lola shows him her arm and turns it, saying, "Goose bumps."

He says, "Here. Out flat." He acts helpless. He says, "For one minute. Please."

One day, Lola, waiting in a check-out line at the grocery store, heard a woman say to another woman, "If a man ever, for any reason, in any way, puts his hand over your mouth and says, 'Listen to me. I have something to say. Be quiet, please.' If he does that, if he says that, scream for a long time and run."

Walt says, "Please, so I can show you."

She squirms down and straightens her legs out, stiffens her arms at her sides. This, she senses, is how it feels on an operating table. This is the terror you fight before the anesthetic hits.

"Thank you," he says. He rolls up the t-shirt she sleeps in and walks two fingers across her stomach. Lola can't take it. His fingers trot from one hip to her other hip, and Walt says, "Ratty's already on stage. What if, when I enter, I loop from here to here?" His fingers move to show her, so she'll feel what Walt's saying, and he scratches her. "Jesus," he says. "An accident. Sorry. You're not bleeding, honest."

She squeezes his hand.

"Oh, God, sorry," he says. He ducks to kiss her stomach, to peck and make better the spot he hurt. If his head were a fish she'd smack it against a rock.

Lola pulls her t-shirt down.

"Acting is acting," Walt says. "Not thinking. You've got to empty your mind. I can't be Toad and spend time thinking, worrying." If he's to be heard, his question is, Should his cross from stage left to stage right be direct or looped? Should he pass in front of Ratty or behind?

Lola says, "I go, and I hear you. I hear every word you say." She does. She sits eight rows up on the aisle. Sticky children crawl all over her, and their parents grab helplessly after them, miss, sit back and whisper to each other. The children say things to Lola, words she can't make out. The first night, all night, she said to them, "Pardon me? What did you say?" They open their grimy hands and offer her candy. Last night, she found a crackerjack stuck to the French braid she'd put her hair in.

Walt stands by the scene he's set up. "If Ratty steps aside like this," Walt says, and he moves the coat rack. "And I step out." He hops to one side. "Then," he says, "then I'd what?"

"You'd be heard," Lola says.

He comes to the bed and swirls the quilt above Lola. It falls on her like the piece of sky it is. Then he is off, toadwalking, saying, "Ratty is left and back, right?" He shifts the coat rack again and lifts the chair. "I'm here," he says and positions the chair directly behind the coat rack.

Lola sees that Walt's gecko is not in its aquarium at the foot of the bed. Or is it? Her glasses are in her purse. The screen on the top of the aquarium is in place, but she can't see the creature. If the gecko is on her anywhere, she'll die. She can't see the cricket Walt fed it last night, but hears it chirp.

Walt sits in the chair and pulls on white socks that come to his knees. His shins are as sharp as plow blades. He says, "I cross straight, keep an eye on Ratty and talk." A week ago, for the play, he had his hair cut flat as an iron. He shaved off his beard, and Lola could not believe how small his face was. Where did Walt go? she thought. What did you do with him? He spoke, and the tiny cream-white face used Walt's voice, but it was like one of those talking heads at the carnival. You put in fifty cents and get your fortune told. She felt like she'd gotten on the wrong bus, like she'd put on someone else's underwear and discovered the mistake too late.

Has the gecko escaped? Lola twists and turns and tries to get a look at her own back. She pats out the quilt and shakes her pillow. No gecko. She wants her contacts, her glasses, x-ray vision.

Walt gets more vitamins, eats them like peanuts, and struts to a window. He says, "I'm in the wing, stage left. My cue, please."

Any line will do. Lola says, "Oh Toad, Oh Toad, Oh Toad."

Where's the gecko? Her contacts? She can't find what she can't see.

Walt does his gadabout Toad. His brow is stormy, and he is saying, "Oh, Ratty, I've blundered terribly. A big awful blunder." He sighs his trademark Toad sigh, and it flip-flops Lola's heart the way stories about lost sheep do. He says, "Oh, Ratty, oh."

Geckos, they're harmless, right? They help out. They eat bugs, and they're quiet pets. You don't have to clean up after them.

"We botch it," Walt says. "Our entrance is off, bad timing, messy blocking, and we can't be heard."

Lola says, "Oh, Vladimirror, what a kettle of fish."

Walt hides his stumpy eyes.

"Vladimirror," she says.

His name for her is Babette. She tends to talk when he talks, and when she does, he says, "No, no, Babette." He says, "No, no, Babette. Your Vladimir, he is talking." It comes out Vladimirror.

He steps up onto the bed, and she stands up. "Babette has gifts," she says. They hug. She sees over his shoulder, high up on the wall, the gecko. She says, "Vladimirror."

"Babette," he says.

"Come," Lola says.

They lie down. Finally, she will be warm. They make tired morning love, and then Walt sleeps, and Lola can't. She never sleeps when she is at Walt's. All night, every night, a streetlight shines in her eyes. Lola has never been able to sleep as long as she has known there is one light on somewhere in the universe. Just before dawn, day after day, she lies in Walt's daybed, and the ceilings assault her. They box the light into terrifying shadows. She's kept her own apartment, the only big thing her lawyer got her out of her divorce, and she'd be there now if its furniture didn't move around at night and trip her, if its walls didn't get in her way, if its windows didn't open on their own.

Every morning, she is on the landing when Charles rolls down his ramp, and every morning, lying in Walt's bed, she hears Charles roll up the ramp. She hears him now, and she says, "Chuck Lightfoot."

After the eight o'clock performance of *Toad of Toad Hall*, Lola and Walt meet Dish and Robin at the Bowlerama. It's a place where they can get drinks and not-bad pizza. Dish is the director and plays Ratty. Robin is Badger, one of the River Bankers, Toad's chum. On stage, she is six layers deep in men's clothes, and her weight lifter's body disappears. Now, in a neon-green Lycra top and black biker's shorts, she glistens. There's no fat on her. She loves to flex her stomach for you.

They find a booth by the pool tables. Maybe six people are bowling, and there is something sad in the noise the ball makes when it hits the lane, something close to despair in the clunk of pins knocking pins down. The bowlers look sickly. Lola listens to Dish and Robin and Walt talk about *Toad of Toad Hall* until her drink comes, then she drifts off. She finds an open pool table, pays for the cue ball, and sets up for the game she calls big suckers and little suckers. What she tries to do is bury the solids and not hit a stripe. There are two rules. She must stand in one place, and she can spot up the cue ball after every shot.

She's close enough to hear Walt say that Toad is a lordly toad. "He's a landowner," Walt says. "Not the butt of jokes."

Dish says, "Toad's full of himself."

"Full of toad feces," Robin says.

"Oh, Robin," Walt says.

She says, "Toad's full of toad."

"A toadload of toad," Dish says.

Lola spears pool balls. You'd think she'd been sent to kill them. She wore high heels, and she likes what they do to her body, the angle the heels make her butt make. She wants Dish to see, and she wants Dish to want her bad.

Walt says, "A lord."

"Toad is stupid about how stupid he is," Dish says. "Play him like that."

In your apartment, at your table, Dish is only Dish. It's the one name he gives out. Whenever he comes by, you think he's come to study you.

"Innocent," Walt says. "Good-hearted, a bit of a clown."

"Wheedling," Dish says.

"But not a toady Toad," Walt says.

Lola racks up a game of nine ball. Her break is weak, is the work of a two-year-old, but she can stop a cue ball cold.

Dish says, "Bombastic. Pompous."

"A gate crasher," Robin says.

Walt sighs his Toad sigh, the one that saddens trees, and he says, "Oh, I'm an ungrateful beast."

"You are," Dish says.

Robin says, "An ungrateful toady beast."

Walt begins to sing "Toad's Last Little Song!" and Dish and Robin join him. It's about panic and howling. It's about the River Bankers retaking Toad Hall. Lola gives up on a five ball she can't get down, pays for her games, and heads for the restroom. Behind her, she hears them singing about smashing windows and crashing in doors, about the chivying of weasels. In the mirror above the sink, Lola sees the woman her husband gave up on. She smooths out the skin around her eyes and tightens her jaw. Her mouth is grim. She's overplucked her eyebrows.

The last weeks she was with her husband, he tailed her. Wherever she was he was nearby. He wasn't sneaky. He stood in the daylight. He was saying, *Here I am.* She remembers him the last time she saw him, his MG under a lamppost in a grocery story parking lot, the top down. He's reading. She walks over and says, "You're the wife in this. You bitch. You nagging two-faced bitch."

And she remembers the first time she saw Walt. He was standing by her husband's car. The hood was up. Two other men were with them. Walt had his beard, a black, curly mask on his face, and he wore a long-sleeved white shirt. His Levi's were ironed, creased. He picked up a wrench, leaned in under the hood, pointed, and tapped something hard. The car revved. The men looked at each other and laughed. Their shoulders shook. They acted like minor gods who'd just sneaked into forbidden territory and tinkered with some universal law.

At night, when the streetlight outside of Walt's apartment won't let her sleep, Lola stands at the window by the bed and expects to see her husband parked under a tree. She always hears what sounds like someone chopping wood blocks away. There is a part of her husband left in Lola's apartment. She can't pin it down, but it's creepy. It's as scary as her fitful heart in her throat.

Lola comes back to the booth, and Robin is up trying to get Dish to leave. Walt says to Lola, "We've concluded Toad is a toad."

"We've drunk to that," Dish says.

Robin helps him up, saying, "Home."

Dish says, "Home."

"Come along?" Robin says to Lola and Walt.

"One more drink?" Walt says.

Dish says, "Not with such a toad." His hair is red and cut into the chopped bristles of an old-world haystack. He's got on dirt-brown peasant trousers and loafers. His shirt is salmon-colored. Dish is six-six, spidery, daddy-longlegged.

"We're gone," Robin says.

It's one A.M. when Lola and Walt climb the stairway to his apartment. Inside, he gets right into unboxing the daybed. He's dropped into a foul mood. On the drive here, she said, "Take me to my place."

"I do, and you'll call me before I get home."

"I won't."

"You will. There will be message on the machine. 'Walt, help. The floor is caving in. There's someone in the bathroom.'"

"I'm not a baby."

"No, you're not."

A block from her apartment, she asked him to stop. She said, "Oh, Vladimirror, turn around. Just one more night at your place. Then I'll be safe."

"You're not handling anything well."

"But I will."

Now Walt's eating vitamins and bad-mouthing Dish. He tries to stand as tall as Dish is, but his clumsy feet boot him off line and into the wrong axis.

He drops onto the bed in his clothes and in five minutes is asleep. Lola sits in the screwy light the window makes on the bed. Here's the best she can do if you want to know what drove her to drive her husband from her. Walt was a means not a reason. She'll tell you her husband's mouth seemed to have been surgically made. She knows how. He is born without a mouth. Doctors consult. They make phone calls and fly in a specialist from Europe, your lunatic-scientist type, blood-shot boiled-egg eyes, weedy hair, shabby clothes, scuffed shoes. You film this in black and white. Nurses pin down the mouthless baby, and the doctor holds up a scalpel. Close up of light glinting off the blade. Close up of the baby's face taut as a balloon. Close up of the nutty doctor. He has gold fillings. He hunches over, grins crazy as a goat, and slices one cut half an inch below the baby's nose and in the shape of a crescent moon.

How, Lola will ask you, can you live day after day with something like that?

Next day, Lola's Chinese green is missing. Walt, sitting on a window sill, lifts one foot and turns it over as if it's not part of him, as if it's a doodad in a gift shop. He says, "Spats."

Lola shops the thrift stores for him. Last week, he asked for vests.

He says, "Where can I get spats?"

She zips his mouth shut and throws away the key. Under a book is the Chinese green. The lid's off, and it's dried out. She can make do. She'll mix colors. She says, "Don't talk." He's dressed for the two o'clock Saturday show, and Lola's making him up. This is theater, but it's semi-pro theater, and there is no money for make-up people. She lays in a moss-green foundation, then blue-green under his eyes. A light green raises his eyebrows into the goggle-eyed look he wants. She mixes a color close to Chinese green and fans it across his cheeks. Her final touch is one red dot in the corner of each eye up against Walt's nose.

She holds up his coat, a black dinner jacket with tails, and he slips into it. She says, "I think I've seen some spats somewhere."

"A perfect touch," he says and shows her one foot.

From the landing on the stairs, Lola waves to Toad as he backs out, and she feels that joy she feels when she sees Santa Claus buzzing along the freeway or pumping gas at a Texaco when it's Christmas. What's it like to see a Toad driving up Main Street in a thirty-thousand-dollar Volvo? Walt acts for fun. He isn't thinking of movies, wouldn't do one if you asked. He doesn't dream of New York. He wants to be in plays in this company in this city. The Sunday "Arts Section" praises what they do, and they travel to states nearby.

The first night Lola stayed at Walt's he gave her a stone he'd found in mountain creek. It was round and as small as a ball you'd use for jacks.

"It's a big marble," she said. "What do they call them, king size?"

He said, "It's not. It's a rock."

"Come on."

"It is," Walt said. "I found it. It's proof of purpose and intention. Of God, if you want."

She gave it back, saying, "Then you keep it. You'll need it."

Below Lola, Charles Rook and Abby come out into in the backyard. Their boy says, "Hit me," and runs out for a pass, and Charles lobs one. The boy hauls it in. Charles stirs vegetables he's had cooking in a wok. He handles the wheelchair easily, spinning it around, tilting it just to the point where it could tip over. Like Robin, he lifts weights. Lola's seen him. Most of the time he's studying up at the university, cancer and radiology, or he's working at a clipping service.

Abby slings the baby out front and high and hangs it in the air like laundry. The baby wiggles, cries. Abby says something to Lola that Lola can't make out.

Lola touches her ear and says, "What?"

Abby sails the baby toward Charles, dive-bombs it at him. Their boy celebrates a touchdown. Charles reaches up, and Abby swings the child past him. Abby walks over to the foot of the iron stairway, turns the baby for Lola to see, and says to her, "Does this look like a mischief machine to you?"

"Not right now."

"Hear that?" Abby says to the baby. She's nose to nose with her child. It's a girl. This is a *National Geographic Special,* and Lola ought to be videotaping it. She should take notes. Somewhere in the shrubs there is a hidden camera, and it is rolling. A voice-over is describing the child-rearing habits of the all-American family. There are lessons here to learn.

Paradise, Lola thinks.

Inside Walt's apartment, she says out loud, "Chuck Lightfoot. His son. His wife. Their baby. We need ducks and lambs and a pond. Choir music."

She feels violent, and she's ugly.

Tonight, at three or maybe four A.M., she'll climb in Walt's ear, ride its tunneling and loop through the semicircular canals until she is sent hurtling into the highway system of his brain, all the way screaming, *Paradise.*

Toad of Toad Hall closes, and the cast comes to Walt's for a party. Charles and Abby open up their two floors. There is cheap wine in cardboard boxes. Walt made pizza. On the front door Lola taped a poster for the show. It's a bad drawing of Walt as Toad. She and Abby hung balloons, and they lined the hallways with glossy cast photos.

Lola is roasting pine nuts in Abby's kitchen when Dish and Robin arrive. They lug in beer. Walt is upstairs showering. There are stairs in the kitchen that lead up to the attic.

Most of the cast is here.

Dish comes in, and Lola shoos him off. He shoos her back.

She says, "Dish."

He says, "Dish."

"Go," she says.

He says, "Away."

She bites her lip, and Dish bites his. "I can do this till I bleed," he says.

Lola says, "Party's out there."

He's close enough to see what she's cooking, and he says, "Pine nuts. I've done that. You didn't know my good-hearted but dirt-poor parents abandoned me in the Pine Nut Mountains. I was raised by Washo Indians."

"You know how to cook pine nuts?"

"You float them in a pan. The bad ones rise. Like eggs."

"Ever go pine nutting?"

"What did I tell you? We lived on rabbit, fish, and pine nuts. I can do pine-nut pilaf, pine-nut corn pudding, even pine-nut cookies."

"You're full of it," Lola says, and she hurries up the stairs to Walt's. She finds her rape whistle in her purse. Walt comes in, his hair wet, drying himself. She says, "Hurry. Everyone's here."

In the kitchen, she outlines the hazards of pine nutting for Dish. The first danger is the needles and the pitch. The needles hurt. The pitch is messy. Then there's the problem of getting lost. You can get caught up in pine nutting, and the desert is about the same no matter where you look—piñons and dirt and rocks. So you carry a whistle. She blows on her rape whistle.

Dish says, "Whoa."

She says, "Then the people you're with can find you. You don't swim alone. You don't pine nut alone."

Robin comes in, hands Dish a beer, and drinks from hers.

Lola blows the whistle. She says, "Pine nutting rules."

Walt has come down the stairs and is standing three or four steps up. Most of the cast is now in the kitchen. Abby's baby is crying, and Charles is outside the doorway. His wheelchair's caught.

Dish says, "Toad."

Walt bows.

"Sing," Robin says.

They break into "Toad's Last Little Song!"

Walt rests his foot on the banister, flashing a silver-toed cowboy boot. He's ironed his Levi's and is wearing a five-hundred-dollar black shirt that belongs on an outlaw. Four vines of embroidered roses climb up its front.

"To Toad," Dish says.

Everyone raises a drink to Walt. Charles wheels in, and Abby hands him the baby, saying, "She's hungry. Just a minute." The baby cries harder. Robin picks Walt up and carries him down the steps into the front room. She drops him on a sofa and says, "Sigh for me, Toad."

This ends in a deep-sigh contest, Walt as judge. He walks around the furniture, listens to everyone's sigh, taps his forehead, tugs at his chin. He sighs Toad's sigh, the measure of all sighs. He picks the chief of the Wild Wooders, whose sigh, Walt claims, reveals the depth of his repentance for all the evil he did and anticipates the good he's now up to.

It's almost midnight when Robin settles in Charles's lap. She's drunk, and she's brought him a beer. "Do you mind?" she says. He looks to Abby.

"Do you?" Robin says to her.

Lola wonders what Charles feels. Is his body capable of anger?

Robin says, "Here's the game." She sips the beer she gave Charles. "I point, and whoever I point to does the scene I set up."

Dish drifts over, says, "Babe—"

"Babe," Robin says. "Babe who?"

"Robin," he says.

"No," she says. "Babe who?"

Dish turns around.

She says, "Babe is not the game. Here's the game. This is it. There is a great deal of hatred in the room, and you're trying to relieve it with kindness." She points at Lola and says, "You're up, doll."

Dish says, "Robin."

"Robin?"

Lola's hands jump to her hair.

Dish says to Robin, "Don't be a drunk and a bitch."

"Bzzzzzzz," she says. "We're looking for kindness. That's not it." She says to Charles, "Am I hurting you? Killing you with kindness?"

Walt says, "Robin."

She says, "Toad. Toadload of toad. Toady Toad." She points at him and says, "Set up. The situation is you are a toad who lives by one simple rule. Walk softly and carry a big stick. Do you carry a big stick, Toady?"

"Enough," Dish says.

Robin says to Lola, "Does he? Does Toad of Toad Hall carry a big stick? A huge stick?"

Lola's crossed her feet and is about to fall down. She untucks her blouse. Maybe she'll blow her rape whistle. Maybe she'll roam around. Maybe she'll find a weapon to use on this nitwit.

Dish tries to get hold of Robin, and she elbows him. She won't let go of Charles. His wheelchair tips, and Walt grabs it just as Charles ducks out of Robin's hammerlock. Abby sits across the room, the baby draped across her legs limp as a towel. It seems as if it's the first time tonight the baby's been quiet.

Dish can't budge Robin. He's in close, and she talks into his neck. She says to Dish, "I'm not hurting *you*, am I?"

Lola's hands won't stop. If they don't, she'll rip buttons from her clothes.

Charles says, "Shhhhhh," and he touches Robin's hair, gathers it up, spreads it out. He traces the line of her chin and softly strokes her neck. He says, "You will live a long and happy life. Wealth, fame, money, headlines—these things are yours if you want them. Your beauty will only increase."

She lets go of Charles, and Dish lifts her from the wheelchair. Dish says, "Time to shut this one down."

By one thirty, Abby and Lola have picked up, Walt has washed the dishes, and Charles has bagged the trash and set it by the backdoor. Walt runs it out to the cans. They say goodnight by the attic stairs, the baby fussy on Helen's hip.

Walt says, "Robin's an ass."

"Aren't we all," Charles says.

Lola says, "Aren't we. Yes."

Walt says, "Our secret's out."

"Amen," Abby says.

Then they all say it. Together, they say, "Amen." Abby hoists the baby up above them and says, "Can you say amen?"

The baby opens her eyes, flays her arms, and is immediately asleep.

"Well," Abby says, "she's only a baby."

Upstairs, the daybed out, Lola lies in the streetlight and hears the sound of wood being chopped somewhere in the neighborhood. At five she hears Charles roll down the ramp and open a trash can. There is the sound his wheelchair makes when he comes up the ramp and the sound it makes when he rolls down it. Up is hollow. Down is solid. It has to do with speed. He comes back up the ramp. Lola knows this scene. He's dressed in his running clothes, his left shoe on his right foot and his right shoe on his left foot. He crosses the patio, and Abby opens the screen door and steps out. She stoops to kiss Charles, and the baby slides off her hip. Lola feels it, almost leaps from Walt's daybed to make a diving save, to scoop up the baby half an inch from the cement. Abby adjusts her weight to the baby's. Charles holds her hand, and Lola understands all of it in her bones. Charles rolls down the ramp, across the grass, and down the driveway into the street.

"Give it up," Lola says out loud.

Walt says, "God. Lola, sleep—won't you?"

"Ah, Vladimirror," she says. "Should I dye my hair the color of a pumpkin?"

"Sleep," he says.

"Should I bob my nose?"

"Sleep first."

"Cap my teeth?"

Walt chucks off the covers and sits almost on top of her. "Color your hair," he says. "Yes. And bob your nose. And cap your teeth. Yes and yes and yes. What—is it your life? You married your father, and little girls do that. They marry their fathers. Your husband was a jerk, a tag-along. My God, your husband looked like you. You married yourself. You were a kid. You did this, and you did that, and your husband did this and that. Then you meet me. And then he takes off. Now you're not a little girl. Daddy is gone and hubby is gone. Now you're an adult. Adults say, 'Shit, damn, I screwed up today. Tomorrow I won't.' But we do."

Has Lola been talking about her father? Did she bring up her husband?

He says, "Now you've had it with me?"

It's the windows. He won't shut them. Anyone could crawl in them. Anyone.

"So," he says, "you shop around," and he rolls off the bed and comes to her side of it. He stands between her and the streetlight and says, "We are all made monkeys of. Somehow, by someone, at sometime. And we make monkeys of people. Look at Robin tonight. What an ass. What a monkey. Maybe you'll make a monkey out of her." He humps his back, bends over, swings his arms across this body, and begins to hop up and down and make monkey noises. He says, "Come on."

He helps her out of bed.

"Monkey see, monkey do," he says.

Lola stands here. Screw Vladimirror.

He climbs onto the bed, reaches for her, and pulls her up. He bounces, and she bounces. The bed will collapse. Lola knows it will. He hops up and down and scratches his head, goes, hoo hoo hoo. "Come on," he says.

Lola's legs buckle.

Walt swings his arms back and forth, grunts, and says, "Monkey see, monkey do."

She swings her arms the way he is.

"Don't think," he says. He picks at his scalp and says, "Empty head."

Soon Lola is doing what Walt does before he does it.

"Empty head," he says.

She'll hold this against Walt.

They scratch their ribs and the top of their heads, and they make monkey noises. Lola and Walt hoot and sway and hop up and down on their curled feet.

Loose in the Mail

My foot is where safety says it belongs on the Toro, and I'm about to yank the engine cord when the mail truck stops in front of the house. There's a thump and a wang from inside the truck, and out jumps the mailman, grinning like a windshield. He vaults the four-foot-high chain link fence and wagging a padded envelope at me takes three mother-may-I giant steps up the lawn.

I block the sun to see him better.

Whisking through the uncut grass, he's saying, "Postage due."

I've put off the first mowing of the spring, mad that a fifty-year-old's got to cut his own grass. Never mind that my two boys are their own adults now and gone from here years ago.

I narrow my eyes and take the mailer.

At the curb, the postman's white box of a truck, engine running, hazard lights blinking, coughs and shudders.

"Two dollars and seventy-three cents," he says.

I squint at the Hawaiian shirt he's wearing tail out over drooping postman's shorts. His black shoes sparkle. Captain ZigZag's tattooed on his forearm. Except for the shipwrecked wired-in-place hippie glasses he's got on, he's one of your radish-faced work-a-day beefy types.

The return address on the mailer is the post office. I say, "Postage due from the post office?"

"Guess so."

"Mind if I take a look?" I say, and I'm mousing through my cut-off Levi's after my pen knife.

"No can do," he says.

The knife's out, snapped open, and I'm ready to pop a staple.

He says, "Pay, then play." His teeth fly around, jitterbug, then snap together. A school bus pulls in behind his truck to let a car coming the other way pass, and Beefy turns around, knobby fists bouncing on his thighs, ready to protect his government property. At the back of his neck a short ponytail sticks out like cut wheat.

Someone's typed "LOOSE IN THE MAIL" on the mailer's label, and my name's misspelled, three d's, not one, E d d d Facer, not Ed Facer. It all adds up to one of a hundred possibilities. Could be something from my youngest boy, who ping-pongs across the U.S. waiting tables, sweeping out zoos, yardworking, doing whatever someone will pay him for. He even sings in a band, which he didn't get from me. Out of the blue, he'll ring the front doorbell, ask for a drink, sleep a night or two in his old room, tell me and the wife stories, then show us his back. He's eighteen.

"Two seventy-three," Beefy says, rocking side to side, his head slung back, checking on his truck. He's chewing gum and is jumpy.

I say, "What if I don't want what's in here? You can understand that. What if it's prayers for hemorrhoids?"

Nothing from Beefy. No smile. Aren't jokes supposed to tear the walls down? Isn't humor the universal language? I could box Beefy's ears. He's a gouty s.o.b., a clod.

I twist the blade under the staple.

He grabs the mailer and whacks it against his leg, saying, "This isn't a store." He tweaks his ponytail, once, twice.

Now someone like you, you can't know what it's like to live here, how short your fuse gets. Beefy's knocking hell out of the mailer and saying something about federal law and how he's going to call nine one one.

"Nine one one?" I say.

"You got you a knife," he says.

"This?" I close the blade shut.

He says, "Two dollars and seventy-three cents up front."

I say, "That's mine."

He backs down the lawn, his nose flared out, the tip of his tongue wiggling on his lower lip.

Short fuses all around.

I say, "Is there some rule?"

Me and this sorehead, this postman—this letter carrier, they call them—we're blue-collar stiffs. He can see it, can't he? Weekdays and weekends, part-time, I hump around a front-end loader when someone happens to see my ad in the *Nifty Nickel*, and I got me a border collie who, when I sit in the one soft chair I own, spreads out across the back of it and plants his snout on my shoulder, me and him doping out on the TV or reading *Newsweek* and the paper, which I plow through, morning after morning, front page to the last want ad. Except the obituaries. I bypass them. I'm teaching the dog poker. He plays two hands and I play two. We get bored, and I work on card tricks.

I bet Beefy's got himself a black lab.

Beefy is about to the fence, and I've followed. I say, "A peek?"

He leaps over.

I say, "Two seventy-three is two seventy-three, and what if it's junk? I got a stapler. We take a look. If I don't want it, we put it back the way it was, the staples right in the old holes."

He says, "You can't have your cake and eat it too."

"Cake?"

"Two dollars and seventy-three cents, yes or no?"

I say, "Profundity's dead, you. Niggling's what's left."

He twirls the mailer and swats at nothing in the air, then steps up into his truck.

"All right," I say.

I try brotherhood.

"Come in," I say. "Here, come down. I'll get the gate open, and we'll stroll up my walkway and inside to drink a cool drink. The wife'll pour. We'll use tongs on the cubes."

In the doorway of his truck, stiff and bolt upright as a damn telephone pole, he says, "I want to finish what I've got to do and get home. Yes or no, you want this?"

I dig out three sweaty dollars from my wallet, wad them up, and toss the ball at him.

"Got no pennies," he says, peeling the dollars apart to count them. He sails a quarter at my head and says, "Owe you two cents."

The coin disappears in the unmown grass.

What my two dollars and seventy-three cents buys me is an address book that one peek tells me is the wife's, the spouse's. She's blind. Did I tell you? Not born that way, but had it come on later and slowly and long before we married. About thirty people from her family are listed in the address book, and the only Facers are our kids. She's put down our youngest's name and then *address unknown.* Every entry is done twice. I write out the names, addresses, and phone numbers, and she punches them in in Braille.

She hasn't told me she lost the book. Not that she has to. We're married, not sewn together at the hip. Her blood flows from Ireland. Mine's German. We're family only because we agreed to be. How I got the book is there's a list of names on a loose piece of paper stuck in the back, and I'm at the top of it, my name spelled E d d d. I don't recognize who wrote it. The ink has that watery fountain pen look. Somehow the book landed in the mail, and there was my name first, so the post office chose me.

A photo I find in the back is of her and our oldest son, who's an odd duck. He wears big loopy sweaters that fit snugly over his hips and button up the front. The buttons look like Lincoln logs. You see him walk, and you think he's knitting his steps. He's tall, but not the seven feet he looks in the photograph. He and the wife—my wife, his mother—are side by side, and he's turned so he can put his arm flat out over her as if it's a publicity shot for the circus. The tallest man in the world meets the shortest woman. His arm's a foot above her. But in real life she's tall, maybe five-seven. On the back it says, Swiss

Days 1983, which explains their clothes, lederhosen and puffy white shirts that look like clouds rolled in and captured them.

You can't really see her eyes in the photograph, but they don't match up. They're the same color, and they're not cross-eyed. The trouble is the pupil in her left eye. It's higher up than the one in her right eye. When you're in close, head-on, her expression says, *I'm listening.* She holds her head that way blind people do. Feeling sorrow, you'd think someone's knocked her around.

We met at a dinner party, and our first date was a drive. She got in my car, rode along, then told me the tires needed to be rotated. "Listen," she said. "Hear that humpa-humpa?" When I asked her to marry me, she said, "I'd like to do this in a kind and gentle way."

I said, "Sounds like a hold-up to me."

She swung her left arm across her body and used one finger to pull down the skin under her right eye. That side of her face looked astonished. She said, "In this eye is love."

I peered in the way you'd search for a stray eyelash.

She crossed her right arm over her left and pulled the skin down under her left eye and said, "In this one is lust."

I could see it.

She said, "I'm fire, and I'm ice, and I lie a lot."

What it added up to was she was saying yes.

When you talk to her, her shoulders lift and drop, and her eyes stay on your mouth. Her eyes are as alive as yours or mine.

I'm hiding the address book from the wife. Don't ask me why. Maybe because she didn't tell me she lost it. Where was she? I wonder. Could the post office tell me? Why doesn't she?

Keeping it is the answer to something. It's more than a game.

What I'm looking for from Beefy is the easy answer of his fist exploding in my face, me crying out and stuttering, "N n ame's E d d d."

There's no one who doesn't know what's happening at post

offices all over the U S of A. Our letter carriers are buying assault rifles and blowing away their supervisors and co-workers, then turning the guns on themselves and making messy holes in their own heads.

I read in the newspaper there's a whole sea of women waiting to heal this planet.

Bring them on is what I say.

One or two of them could start with me and Beefy. I've left the grass uncut, the mower by the porch, and his quarter to rot.

My dog—I call him Marvel, which is short for Marvelous—and me, we'll be sitting on the porch, me dealing Hold'em or doing magic, and we'll see Beefy across the road, him walking up a driveway, his stingy body moving like someone's opened his fly, yanked out his dong, taken a good grip on it, and is leading him along the way you'd pull a kid's red wagon along the street.

Every day I put a letter in the mailbox for him to pick up. No stamp on it. I'm writing to names in the wife's address book. I lugged out an old manual typewriter I owned in high school. I picked up classy paper and envelopes and found dead center on the carriage. I type I KNOW WHO YOU ARE. Then add a name, like Mildred, the wife's mother. The print's like a bumpy road. On a brother-in-law's, I wrote I SAW WHAT YOU DID WITH RUBBER AND I KNOW WHO YOU ARE, STANLEY. I'd pay to be a fly on the wall when he opens it and blinks the way he does.

Who am I kidding? They'll check the postmark. They'll phone the wife and say, "What's up?"

She'll say, "Up?"

"Everything okay?" they'll say.

"Shouldn't it be?" she'll say.

She and they, they'll discuss the possibilities. Who could be doing this? It's got to be someone who watches them. She'll stick closer to me. If she could see me, she'd begin to study me out of the corner of an eye.

She's heard me typing. What bothers me is the irrational, the fear that she knows what key I've hit, what letter I've typed, like in the old spy movies when the bad double agent is phoning the boss, and the good double agent zeros in on the clicks those old dial telephones used to make. He's able to memorize the number. She's asked, and I've told her I'm starting a diary. Short, to-the-point entries, I tell her. Days summed up in one word. That ought to hold her and worry her some.

Marvel and me keep to our side of the fence when Beefy pulls up. He'll pluck out a letter, turn it over, and his ponytail twitches. His juicy lips suck then unsuck. He's got three choices. He can send it postage due, or toss it. God bless him if he tosses it. That'd be a vote for sanity. His final choice, as I see it, is he can say to me and my gentle dog, "No stamp, pisshead."

To which, I'd say, "Name's E d d d."

He needs to know I'm worldy-wise.

Day after day he drives off.

My belief is we don't see people in direct sunlight enough.

I'm loafing here on the porch steps, working on card tricks, and Marvel is herding sheep in his head, snout in the wind then plugged into shrubbery.

The wife comes out, feels her way down two steps, and touches me.

"Give me a pat," I say and lean my head toward her.

She does.

I say, "I feel better."

She says, "The lawn's getting high."

Has she knelt down and felt it? I'd bet not. She knows. She just does.

"I'll get to it," I say.

She pats me again and says, "I've mussed your hair."

I describe Marvel, and she nods. I get my pen knife out and hand it to her open, and I say, "Magic." I shuffle the cards and ask her to pick one. She's feeling how sharp the knife is. I guide her hand to the deck.

"Don't let me see it," I say.

She holds the card she's drawn flat against her chest, and we begin to see there's a basic problem here.

I say, "Guess I'll have to see it."

She turns it over and says, "What is it?"

"Seven of spades." I have her put it back in the deck. I say, "I happen to have this paper napkin on me and I'm wrapping it around the deck."

She says, "Just happen to have—right?"

When I'm done, she checks out the napkin, makes sure it surrounds the cards. I say, "You run the knife into the deck." I help her. We leave the blade stuck in there, and I say, "Name your card, the one you drew."

She says, "The seven of spades."

Now on the stupidity scale of one to ten we've gotten ourselves caught up in a ten. I tear the napkin away and cut the deck where the knife is. Her card is under the blade, the seven of spades. I say, "It's the seven of spades."

She says, "Ta-dum."

I close up the knife.

She uses my shoulder to help her stand up, and Marvel turns around to see her. She sways on the porch. She says, "If I could see, I'd drive across country on the back roads, and I'd stop at every cafe and lookout point."

"Would I be by your side?" I say.

She says, "We'd take Marvel along."

I say, "You okay?"

"Me?" she says.

"You."

She says, "Maybe you can show me that trick in the afterlife when I get my eyes back."

I'm one breath away from telling her I've got her address book.

She says, "The mail's coming."

I hear her open the screen, then shut it, and the front door closes.

Beefy's truck stops out front, and he swings through the

gate and comes up the walkway. He says, "Peace," and flashes me the sign for it.

"Come in," I say.

And he does, even pets the dog. The wife's at the sink. They say hello. She turns around and half shuts her eyes and tilts her head back the way she does so that you'd swear there is one pinpoint of light she's seeing everything in. Her tall white cane's by the front door.

When I hand him his cool drink, Beefy slips me the two cents he owes me and like it's a dirty joke between us says, "That mailer—what was in it?"

"Ain't opened it," I say.

He tweaks his ponytail in the way I'd like to video tape.

Now there's a fib between me and Beefy.

I say, "Want to do the honors?" and act like I'm getting up to dig the mailer out.

"None of my business, is it?" he says.

"Probably not." I'm shuffling my trick cards. I tell Beefy that Texas Dolly Brunson says poker is about people. You got to know what makes the other guy tick. I say, "You need to get inside your opponent's head." I'm quoting Texas Dolly.

Beefy sips his drink.

I shuffle the deck so he can see the cards, and I say, "See, it's an ordinary deck."

He nods, then takes off his wire glasses and rubs his eyes.

I say, "Hold up your finger" and raise my index finger.

He puts his up.

"Poke your finger in and stop my shuffle anytime," I say.

He does.

I lift off the top half of the deck and tell him to look at the card under his finger. I say, "Now put it back." I cut the cards. I shuffle them. I ask him to cut and shuffle. Then I cut them one last time. I pick the card off the top of the deck and say, "This could be your card, but that'd be too easy. I could have palmed it." I ask him if it's the card he chose.

He says, "No."

I show him the second card, the seven of spades, and say, "This is your card, right?"

"It is," he says. He takes a big drink.

"I cheated," I say. "It's not magic."

"Tell me how," he says.

I sense the wife behind me. There's a way she stands in the alcove that reminds me of movies I've seen. She's perfected the blind way of standing, that way that is defiant yet jittery, the way that shows she's waiting for a voice she recognizes or for the particular fall of my footstep.

I say to Beefy, "Can't do it. I took an oath."

"Do the trick again," Beefy says.

"Not today."

I hear the wife slipfooting her way toward the bathroom. I say to Beefy, "Were you entertained?"

"I was," he says and sets his drink down. He wipes his hands on his postman's shorts.

"Mystified?" I say.

He says, "That's possible."

When he leaves, Beefy squinches up his eyes and says, "Have we got some kind of truce?"

"I think we do," I say.

I walk him out, and at the gate, I say, "You got you a dog?"

"Sure do."

"A lab?" I say. Marvel's pasted himself to my leg.

Beefy says, "Is there another kind?"

I say, "Black?"

He says, "Black."

I get the address book from a side drawer where I've hidden it. At the typewriter, I knock out one more letter. It says,

DEAR SEVEN-FOOT MAN,
HOW'S THE WEATHER UP THERE?

I address it to our oldest boy and lick a stamp for the envelope. If I was to tell anyone about the letters, it'd be our youngest boy. He'd tell me one of his stories, and I'd tell him mine. I carry the typewriter to its dusty spot in the cellar and put my supplies in a cabinet.

Here's my problem for that army of women out there who are set to heal this planet. How do I get my wife's book to her?

The typing will stop, the letters will stop, and they'll know. They'll put two and two together.

Do I put the address book where she's kept it all these years and let her find it one day?

I don't have a clue to the kind of hand she's holding. She's a poker face. You can't read her mood. Beefy, he's a loser, a small fry. He couldn't take a pot if he drew three aces to one he's kept. Me, I've spent my life drawing to inside straights. You get one, and what have you got? A winning hand? Probably, ninety-nine out of one hundred deals. It's the one hundredth that nails you.

Do I meet the wife face-to-face and slip her address book into her hand and tell her what I've been up to?

You know that look the blind get, the tilt of the head that says, *Is that someone at the door?* The wife, she does that a lot.

According to Texas Dolly a man's true character comes out in a game of high stakes poker. You can't hide from it. I'm quoting Dolly.

Truth is I'm not sure anymore I know what game it is we're playing. Or who is in, who's anteed.

Is that army of women organized? I hope so.

Me? I'm whistling in the dark.

As Long As Lust Is Short

Kay pooches her lips out and sulky to mimic the fish lips of the women in the magazine she's brought along. She says, "You don't want me to weigh my words, do you?"

I wouldn't mind.

I've just said, *Do I need to hear this?*

She's come by my office to pick me up and is telling me about her lust for Gary, a guy I work with. Weighing your words means your marriage is false coin. She curls her magazine up and taps my ribs, then slips around behind me, saying, "Just a little lust." One of her polished nails glides along the bone of my hip. She says, "This part on a man drives me crazy." Gary's hips do it for her.

We're married a year, and I'm learning.

She says, "When I think of his hair I could puke."

He has hair like a wallet. I dial the one call I need to make. Outside, sprinklers chug along. Traffic settles at a red light.

She says, "I'd like to forget I've ever seen the back of his head."

It's after six, and I'm getting no answer on the phone.

"He's such a schoolboy," Kay says. "Horny as a nephew."

"He's a troll," I say.

"God, yes," she says. "He's a squirt. I couldn't take more than two minutes of him."

"As long as lust is short," I say, and I hang up the phone. I write the number down, then snap my briefcase closed. I have one letter to look over. If we're not gone in one minute, Gary'll be plugged into my doorway, throbbing, jacked onto the toes of his lazy shoes, saying what he says at some point nine days out of ten, which is, "Wish I fucked as much as you sell." Talking like that in front of Kay juices him up the way it would a ten-year-old. He'll say something he thinks is crude as long as his back's to her, and he won't look up until someone else speaks. Half the time he's in a room with Kay, his eyes are on her chest.

We sell insurance, mostly auto. I've transferred from Denver to Salt Lake City and will be here a year or two. I'm not upper management, and I'm not a salesman. I sell because to produce producers you produce, which is why I've been sent here. I'm your get-that-place-in-shape man. Business comes to me. Mostly it's people telling people I'm a straight shooter, and it's me talking fast and being a handshaker. And I'm to the point and as honest as I'm allowed. I've been to colleges and dress right. I can use the word *diffident* and know what I said.

Kay has picked up the framed picture I have of her and me, and I'm rewording a letter. Kay says, "It's not like I'd do anything about it."

"Gary?" I say, and he is in the doorway, rumbling his knuckles on the frame and saying to Kay, "Did I tell you I'm an orphan?"

She chews at a fingernail wickedly.

"No loving mom, no forceful-yet-endearing pop," he says and skips over close enough to pull her hand away from her mouth and say, "Don't."

She might slug him.

"Your death," he says, and he's hung onto her hand. "Pretty color, but death by nail polish is a real medical fact."

She gives him fish lips, pulls her hand away, and goes back to biting her nails.

He turns to me, acting hangdogged, and says, "Her funeral. Brain dies, slow and agonizing. First sign is she'll wear gloves and a wool hat when it's 110 degrees. Then no bra year round. Tits'll be popping out right and left." *Tits* puffs him up, sends him around my desk like a slippery child, his shoes whistling on the carpet. His suit coat flaps back, and the lining is the same blue as his eyes. His tie's got the identical blue in it. He can see we're headed out, and he's wild to hold us here. "Tonight," he says. "Dinner at our place and games. That trivial one."

Kay's chomping one nail.

Tick, I hear.

"Can we call you?" I say. "Got two people to reach and I may need to go over and see one claim."

"Call me?" he says. "Get back to me?" He yanks one of his business cards from his vest and says to me, "Top number's the office. Bottom is home." He's mad. In cartoons smoke'd be billowing from his ears. He's a fiddler who's blown a string getting into a tune. "Can you call me?" he says. "Why not? Day or night. Hey, I'm here to serve you." So close we're in contact, he bumps my hip with his, twists away, and says, "You've got my number."

"Okay," I say. "All right."

"All right," he says and pretends to toss something in the air and hit it. Must be tennis. He dips through a backhand, then sets up for a drop shot. He says, "Game set match." His suit opens on its blue lining.

Kay's come up next to me, and I say to her, "Okay with you?"

"Maybe," she says. She's gnawing a nail and tapping me with her magazine.

Gary says, "You're dead," and he points at her chewing, then erupts, hitting backhands and forehands and overheads.

I say, "We'll be there at seven."

Kay says, "Maybe."

"Seven," he says. "Home address is on the card."

I say, "Seven."

He's out the door and we hear him on the phone in his office.

Kay says, "Sleaze ball."

Smarmy's the word I'm thinking.

We've been home, I've showered and made my phone calls, and now Kay and I are in a slowdown on the freeway, already half an hour late to Gary's. There's an accident up ahead.

"Cowboys," Kay says. "Don't get me started on cowboys."

What's triggered this, I think, is our slide past a black pickup, one of those that sit thirty feet up in the air on ten-foot-tall shiny black tires. I missed seeing the driver, but angle the rearview and spot one of those straw cowboy hats on the dash, a disgruntled mustache drooping down a narrow face and creeping along the jaw, a splattering of hawk feathers bursting from his rearview mirror. Something about all of it says war.

"God," she says, "you're young, and you want what's in their pants."

I say, "Do I need to hear this?"

"And when they want you," she says, "when they want what you can give them, nobody can be sweeter. Nobody can talk you up like a cowboy. You'll take the shit on the boots, the K-Mart shirts with those pearl snaps, the Copenhagen in their pocket. They smell different. They don't smell like you and me."

Up till now, the only cowboy I've heard about is one who tossed her from one Montana border to every other Montana border like the state was a bandbox. She'd rolled awake one morning and eyeballing his face concluded she was in bed with tempestuous and maybe fatal weather. She said *good-bye* only after the door to his trailer had ticked shut and she was on the road, a tape of Emmylou Harris clarifying what Kay was feeling, which had to do with lust and rotten love and what she'd been told about screwballs when she was a child.

"Cowboys've got the walk," she says. "Then there's all the shit that goes along with it. All the tooling on their belts, their name on the back. Can you believe it? I had one named Doug. There it was on the back of his belt, Doug dyed in red. He wanted me to call him Douggie. This is a fact. Douggie. I didn't. I'd say, 'Doug-ga-las.' When he was good, and he could be good, I'd stick a finger through his pants loop and stay put or be jerked wherever he was off to."

A freeway exit drops us into Gary's subdivision, and I ask her what the address is.

She tells me, then says, "Their shirts. I'm serious. They buy them at K-Mart."

I'm as far as you get from a cowboy.

Finally, I say, "Do I need to know this?"

"Take my word for it. You want to hear this," she says.

"We're trading stories?"

"Partly."

"Sounds promising," I say.

"Ain't all God's truth," she says.

We're looking for a cul-de-sac. I turn a corner, and I say, "The one who bought you the house, he was a cowboy or the one who tried to be a cowboy?"

"For me, he tried to be," she says. "He'd wear Levi's, then I got him into Wranglers. He'd get a new pair, soak them in the tub, and put a crease down the front or roll the bottom. He got it wrong. He had the belt and his name on the back. Jacob. But he was a dude. He'd buy cowboy-looking shirts at the store where the college kids bought clothes."

"Could he do the walk?" I say. She's done the cowboy walk for me.

"No," she says. "He'd do it and end up looking like he'd stepped in shit."

Cowboys, she's told me, walk like their feet hurt, like they're sore from doing things that'd kill a normal man. Their walk says if you'll give them half a minute to sit and rest, they'll get up and do something legendary.

What I've heard from her is the man bought her a house, only he didn't tell her it was for her. He said his family got it for his sister. She'd dated him over a year, and together they painted the place inside and out and replaced windows. They'd sit on the porch at night. Then one day he let the secret out—it's to be your house, honey—and gave her a ring, which she held onto and which almost killed her when she was driving home staring at it sitting next to her. She almost dumped herself and her Jeep in a ditch. When she gave it back, they were at the house, and she said, "I don't know what I want, but I want something, and this isn't it." She had to explain she didn't mean the house. She meant him. He picked her up and locked her inside. She was there for hours until a friend of his came by and let her out. She tells me if she had married the guy, she'd have had an affair with the friend who helped her. Not because he helped her. She'd had the hots for him all along. She was planning it. She'd be painting a room in the house, and she'd be figuring out how she'd sneak around, how she'd lie, and where she and the friend would do it.

We find Gary's, a white brick house. The porch is lit up, and lights along a cement path show us how to get to the front door. The grass is cut so short it looks like a pond.

We're about to the door when Kay says, "What's that bumper sticker? Cowboy's Stay on Longer and Ride Harder?"

"I'll pick one up," I say.

"Here's a joke for you. Try it out at the office. Tell it to Gary," she says. "Why do cowboys have their name on the back of their belts?"

I think I can guess.

She says, "So when they finally get their head out of their ass they'll know who they are."

We've opened a little gate to Gary's yard.

I say, "The wine." We brought a bottle, and I left it in the car. I jog back for it.

Coming up the walk, I see Gary has come out and met Kay. He's trying to hug her. She steps back, points at me, and says, "Forgot the wine."

Gary can't be stopped. He kisses her and shoves a hand in my direction. I take it, and I show him the wine. I'm in a tie, and he's in a golf shirt.

"Nice," he says.

Something's wrong, and it's not the tie.

His wife has come out. She could be our mother, her hair, her lipstick, her shoes. She's got a beehive hairdo that seems to have been sat on, and her shoes are cloth slippers. Her lipstick's half eaten away. Gary hugs her and says, "Should have told you we don't drink."

Kay says, "Wine isn't drinking."

"And we don't have drink in our house," Gary's wife says.

Gary says, "Bring it in. We'll keep it in the refrigerator, and you take it when you leave."

I say, "Let me just put it in the car."

He relaxes.

His wife's name is Olive. Inside, she disappears, and Gary leads us into a family room. There is a huge TV, and the fireplace opens on both sides. You can see through it into the dining room. On the other side, Olive's legs pass by, then return. Gary asks us if we'd like some apple juice.

"Love it," I say.

Kay, nibbling a fingernail, shakes her head no.

When he's gone, two children appear at the end of the hall. One, a boy, says, "I'm Elmo."

Kay says, "Hi," and the kids run away. There's a cat Kay's trying to coax over. She says to me, "No wonder Gary talks dirty."

"Not in this house," I say. No way would he say *Wish I fucked as much as you sell* with Olive on the same block with him.

Kay says, "Here, kitty. Kitty kitty."

The room is dark and cold, and children take turns hurrying by and into the kitchen, then they fly up stairs and race down the hallway. The cat took off after one of them. Rock music is playing in a back room.

Above the fireplace are trophies, and next to them are cut glass figures of Venus emerging from the sea. One of them shows her riding the waves. There is a row of bronze owls, ranging from baby to adult, and on the skirting of the fireplace is a plywood butler. Maybe he's a valet. Whatever he is, he's holding a tray of mints.

There is a blond piano, and above it are photographs of Gary and Olive and six children. There is also a picture of Jesus in a blue robe, his arms poking straight out from his sides like he's spinning himself through a game of All Fall Down and trying to keep his balance. There's a nimbus lighting up his head. I think of a man I heard talking in an elevator. This guy's wife replaced his picture on their nightstand with a picture of Jesus. The man in the elevator was saying to a buddy, "What do you do about something like that?"

Gary steps from behind the fireplace, holding a jug of apple juice, and says, "Might as well have this with dinner. It's ready."

He pours me some juice and shows Kay where to sit. The table is round, and we are placed like the four points of a compass. We help ourselves to the food. I'm passing Kay rolls when Gary says to me, "I'm moonlighting, selling Mason shoes."

"Mason?" I say. "Is that something different?"

"Air cushioned innersole," he says. "It's an outfit out of Wisconsin. Came in the mail. I'll show you after we eat."

It's okay with me.

He's got a card on him they sent. It shines like one of those AAA bumper stickers. His name's on it, authorizing him to be a Mason Shoe Man. He says, "It pays some bills. Milk alone comes to a thousand a month. We've got number seven coming along," and he looks at Olive, who is putting a potato-and-bean mix on his plate.

Her hair in the kitchen light? It looks like it leapt from a bush and attacked her.

Kay says, "What about your kids?"

"Our children?" Olive says.

"About eating," Kay says.

"The children ate earlier," Olive says.

Gary says, "We usually eat around six."

I stop myself from saying I'm sorry we were late. It's a useless thing to bring up.

We eat, and Gary talks about Mason shoes and how kids wear things out. He keeps shifting in his chair, then actually turning in it until he's got his back to Olive and is talking only to Kay. Small talk dead-ends on him, and he says to her, "I told you I'm an orphan."

Olive says, "Potatoes?" and holds them up. All she gets is the back of Gary's head. I take the bowl from her, and I'm passing it along when Gary intercepts it and starts to spoon a helping out for Kay.

"I can do it," she says. "I'm strong." She sets the bowl on the table, rolls up her sleeve, and flashes a bicep at him.

He reaches out to squeeze it, and she shifts so he can't.

Gary says to her, "To make a short story long, I was a baby when my father and mother, out for a drive or going to the store—no one knows really what they were doing—ended up waiting at a light, and when it turned green, the car in front didn't move, so my father honked. I'm told I was in the backseat on a blanket. A man gets out of the car and comes back, and a witness who saw all this says he said, 'Get off my ass,' and shot my father in the head. Then he shoots my mother and drives off. This is in a small town, not some big city, and it's thirty years ago. They sent me to my mother's parents, and they died when I was seven." All the time Gary is talking, he is leaning toward Kay, and behind him, Olive is giving me food to pass along. She'll show me a bowl or a plate and tilt her head to ask, *More?* Gary comes to the end of his story and says, "So that's the sad tale of how I am an orphan." His left hand has come to rest on Kay's butt. I don't see him do this because of the table, but later she'll tell me, her fingers showing my butt just the spot he was touching.

Kay glances up at Olive, stops eating, and, her mouth two inches from Gary's, says, "Gary, get your lips off the dish."

"What?" he says.

I'd have bought tickets for this.

"Back off," she says.

He sits up, saying, "I was only—"

She says, "What did the man say to your dad? Get off my ass? Is that what he said?" She pinches her nose, which is her way of telling you you're treating her the way men treat women in China, and it stinks.

Olive, juggling a pitcher of milk she's about dropped, says, "Kay." She's the mother whose son's been misunderstood.

"You too," Kay says, pointing a fork at Olive, then she's banged her chair back and is headed for the front door.

Gary turns to me, then Olive, who is wiggling herself out of her chair. Kay's gone and has left the front door open behind her. Gary and I end up in the entryway, and the cat is following Kay. Olive says, "Don't let the cat out."

Too late.

A teenage girl, maybe fifteen, is standing at the end of the hallway, wearing a t-shirt big enough for a six-foot fat man, and her eyebrows make little black sabers. Her hair spurts up and out like the top of a palm tree. She goes after the cat.

Gary says, "What'd I do? I was just telling a story."

I say, "Baseball talk, Gary."

"Baseball?"

"Get your lips off the dish. It's what a pitcher is saying to a hitter when he throws a fastball at the hitter's head, when he knocks him down. It's the brush-back pitch. In a way it's a compliment."

"I'm the hitter."

"You're the hitter."

Olive has come up behind Gary. The night's spoiled. Her eyes look like tattoos. Things have not gone right for her boy.

Gary offers his hand to me, and I say, "It's Kay's you need. Her IQ runs circles around yours."

His daughter carries the cat in. Three other children spill out of the hall.

Gary says to them, "What's going on here is not your business."

I leave his handshake in the air like a model plane.

He says, "No hard feelings."

"That's possible," I say. "But you're not dealing with me."

"The Whip," Kay says. She's gulping wine. The Whip is a bar out in the country between the city and one of the towns it feeds. We're okay there because we're not from here. We drink at the bar and dance slow. We're not city people out to study the local riffraff, out to see how the lowlifes get along.

I say, "Get your lips off the dish?"

"Been waiting years to use that," she says.

In the dark, in the car, she slugs wine down and looks at me cockeyed. You ever seen the eyes on an Australian sheep dog?

Hers glow like that. You wouldn't want to sleep in a room with them. She's had half the bottle. We're out of the city on the winding road that runs past The Whip. Maybe I'm doing fifty. I come to a turn, and Kay, the wine bottle on the seat between her legs, says, "Bite it off."

She means the turn. I cut into it, and the car slams left like someone's kicked it. Next turn, the wine bottle swinging between her thumb and a finger, she says, "Take a bite out of it. Feel the road."

I do.

"Yes," she says and, taking the wheel, passes me the wine. We're doing sixty. "Never push," she says. "Only pull," and she is showing me how, wheeling us through a turn that's posted at forty-five, that's preceded by one of those signs that say SLIPPERY WHEN WET and illustrate the danger with a curvy line.

She lets go, sits on her feet, and finishes the wine. Next turn, holding the bottle like a spyglass, she says, "Take a straight line through it."

I am. We're doing seventy.

"Hold it, hold it," she says.

I hold it.

Up ahead is The Whip. Its portable sign, light bulbs blinking around it, says LIVE MUSIC TONIGHT THE WASHBOARD SISTERS. We hear their twang as we fly by.

"Fasten up," I say.

"What?"

"Your belt."

She drops the bottle and snaps her belt on.

I say, "Mine."

She helps me into it.

We're doing eighty on a thin straight strip of two-lane highway.

I jump on the brake and crank the wheel, throw the world around us like a carnival ride, then cut the headlights and let the smoke and dust crawl and fan out while we idle and wait before we head for The Whip. The wine bottle's loose on the floor.

Kay's eyes flare up.

Inside The Whip, Kay locates a booth, and I get two beers. When I find where Kay is, some tall old cowboy is resting on our table and talking to her. He's got his hat in his hand behind his back, and there it is on his belt, his name, Jed.

I arrive to hear her say to him, "Maybe later."

He's given her one of those boxes of candy you win by punching holes on a board, and he asked her to dance. She told him her first dance goes to her husband.

So, we dance, and she hooks a finger through the belt loop above my hip, and I smell the wine. The Washboard Sisters sing about cowboys. It's the one love song they know by heart.

I dip Kay and whisper to her. I say, "And who gets the second dance?" Getting up out of our booth, I had curled my finger into a beer bottle and picked it up that way. Now it sits on Kay's butt, bouncing a little, keeping three-quarter time with the Washboard Sisters, who are singing an old Hank Williams's tune. In Kay's ear, I ask Hank's cowboy questions about why and how, I talk hard and sad about love and tears.

Hops

Coin's daughter Nadine takes Coin's free hand and tells Coin about the world. The world has a dry voice, she says. She makes her voice dry and says her name.

Nadine is twenty-three.

Coin says her name, and he keeps her hand in his.

"Hops," she says. "Call me Hops."

Hops is a stuffed frog Coin bought Nadine years ago. She wore it out and has kept it around, has tied a red bandanna around its neck to keep its froggy head from sitting in its froggy lap. Hops is two shades of avocado and wears a cloak-and-dagger grin.

Nadine and Coin are circling a pond in the Sculpture Garden at the Museum of Modern Art. She has always walked as if every step she takes is the first she has ever taken. There is something wacky about Nadine's feet and odd in the set of her arms. She stops and admires a weighty sculpture, a ponderous Henry Moore. She swings Coin's arm. She says, "The world acts good-hearted. The world comes by and says hello. At parties, the world takes you aside. It has gotten you a drink. It lends you its tapes. You bring the world home, and it sits on your couch where it crosses its legs at the knee."

Nadine's sorrow is the sorrow of birds.

She is wearing a fifteen-hundred-dollar plum-colored cloth coat. Her skirt is black, and her shoes are tobacco brown. They're hightops. They have eyelets. White lace rises from each shoe and circles her ankles like doll collars. On her black sweater, she has pinned a red enamel heart where her heart is.

Nadine brings their hands up and holds them to Coin's chin. She tests Coin's grip. She says, "Arm wrestle?" She has her mother's mouth, her mother's eyes, and her mother's ears. Where does Coin fit in?

"Your baby is having a baby," Nadine says. She lets go of Coin and shifts a black iron chair around. She sits down, saying, "And I don't want it."

Coin tries to find the sky. What he sees is blue and firm. He bumps Picasso's *She-Goat.*

His heart's in his mouth.

Nadine married Coin's friend Michael. Michael is forty-two and has two ex-wives and five children, two in the city, one in Maine, one in college, and one on the drift. He and Coin own a restaurant they run.

Nadine says, "I always sit like this now." Her coat is open, and her knees show. She says, "Like I'm about to stand." She goes into her pocket and comes up with a cigar. Here, turning in her fingers, it surprises her. She says, "Coin, a fine cigar." She holds it up like a scientist.

She offers it to Coin, saying, "It's yours. Have it. It's a find."

She hunts in her pocket for what it was she was after and finds a deck of cards. She says, "Rook." On the box, a rook holds the hand it's been dealt.

Coin says, "Tennessee for Two." He can't unwrap the cigar.

Nadine says, "Kentucky Discard. Do you pass? I pass. Little Sweep and Big Sweep. My bid?" She opens the Rook box and says, "Few people know Rook, Coin. I sit close to strangers at the depot, on park benches, and I talk them into games. Teach me, they say. I have to."

Coin gives up on the cigar wrapper.

She says, "Play? You and me, one game for the championship of the world."

"No time," Coin says, and he buries the cigar in his overcoat. He helps Nadine up, steadies her in front of him, and says, "Why are we here?"

She says, "Does Michael need six children? Does he want them coast to coast? Sea to shining sea?" She takes big steps around Picasso's *She-Goat,* in sunlight, her arms crossed high up on her chest.

When was it they had said all it was they were going to say to each other?

Outside, near her subway stop, Coin buys Nadine rum balls, and she has the sack open before he's paid.

He says, "Nadine." He ducks to find her eyes, saying, "May I call you Nadine?"

"Hops," she says. "Hops has character. Hops tells you something."

Coin's heart skids and bangs around. It's a one-man band in his chest.

Nadine says, "I don't want anything to do with babies." She rolls a rum ball into her mouth and wiggles her sticky finger's near Coin's face, teasing him and looking for help. She says, "Babies. Yuck."

He gives her a handkerchief.

She says, "Coin, you need your beard. You wore it like an explosion." She makes bomb noises.

Coin cups his hands around his mouth and spreads them as if he is about to call for help.

The story Michael tells is he was raised by wolves, not in some folktale way, but in real life. His hair is always knocked back in some kind of wet geometry. His eyes are negligent, and his beard is a schnauzer's beard. He's got the Vietnam War under his belt. He came home and sold options twenty-four hours a day until he got rich.

Now mornings he's down on Amsterdam Avenue in pickup basketball games. His hook's his ticket. It's an urgent wounded thing that can't be stopped.

When Nadine is where Michael is she comes up like she's going to stand on his feet, and she puts her face in his face and talks his ear off.

Michael, at the bar, is gnawing on a pencil and looking at a woman when Coin comes in. She's across the room at a table. Michael'd like to be doing a cigarette ad. The woman is reading a box, turning it over and over, slowly, as if it is a light bulb that has burned out. It's noon, and she is dressed for night. Her high heels sit like crows on the floor. Coin picks up a sandwich and asks for coffee. He and Michael locate a table three feet away from the woman. Michael says, "Hello," and the woman studies the box. Michael says to Coin, "Her teeth."

The woman slams the box down and begins treating her hair violently. She's wrecking it.

Michael says, "One word, Coin." He taps his pencil's erasure against his teeth. "For white. For the white of her teeth. One word."

The box sits on the woman's table, and she bangs a fist down on each side of it. Her hair has become a weedy hillside, like a van Gogh. She looks as if she is mad enough to eat the box.

Michael tucks his chin under and picks his feet off the ground. They pedal, bobbing and weaving, hurried. He's a man too big for the tricycle he's on. He says, "Pearls. Virginal."

Coin unwraps the pickles he brought along, then thumps his tie where his heart is and says, "Pit-a-pat. Pit-a-pat. True love." He taps his heart, says, "Pit-a-pat."

Michael says, "Save me, Coin. Help." He's bowed his head, and his feet have stopped. He's left with a foot on a foot.

Coin says, "Ivory. Snow-capped. Alabaster."

Michael's eyes are hasty beebees. His feet are flat irons.

"Orchids," Coin says.

The woman lifts the box, only her fingertips touching it, and she undoes the lid, pulls up and out four tiny white triangles and removes a porcelain bird.

A tall woman, talking fast, comes in and sits at the woman's table. She is saying, "Paul Anka is alive and performing tonight." The woman Michael has been eyeing hands the tall woman the box, but keeps the bird. It's a robin. The tall woman takes the bird. She says, "God, don't you love it. Paul Anka. Alive." She can't fit the bird in the box. She says, "Didn't you think he was dead? Shot in Reno." She turns the robin over and searches its face, says to the bird, "You look swell."

Michael scoots over, and they turn to look at him. He is saying something about Paul Anka.

Coin calculates what it would take to fall. If he tipped his chair this way or that, at what point would the gravity that taxes us toss him to the floor? He thinks of Nadine's story, of Nadine in Michael's face like a minor storm.

Coin remembers a pumpkin-colored violin resting on Nadine's shoulder and his clumsy hands trying to help, and he taps his heart, thinking, Pit-a-pat. Pit-a-pat.

Michael says, "Here's what I am told, Coin. It's her body. That's what I hear. I hear that day in and day out. Nadine says, 'Whose body?' I say, 'Yours.' She says, 'I rest my case.'"

Coin says, "Meaning."

"Meaning," Michael says, "meaning it's her body. It's Nadine's baby. She says to me, 'What did you do that was so hard? Did you do something that cost you anything?' She says, 'You have five. Do you need six?' I'm to keep in mind this is her baby. I'm not to forget that. It's a fact."

Coin says, "So you abort it?"

"Me? You forgot, Coin. It's her body. It's her baby. You're not to forget that. She'll remind you."

Michael is standing, and Coin is sitting. Michael is trim. He says, "I'm not Superman, am I?"

They go run in the dark city, up Columbus, away from the park, and anger sits on Coin's chest. Michael, a yard out front, paces him. He has that war under his belt. Besides, his legs are stringy.

They're in street shoes. Coin flips off cars, and obscene words erupt from him. His anger struts like an imp. He runs a cab into oncoming traffic.

His feet are rocks.

Nadine takes bumpy train rides into New England. She goes to sales and closeouts and hopes the poor will jab their pointy elbows in her belly.

Michael finds her day after day on top of the refrigerator,

crouched down up there, her head two inches from the ceiling, her knees up around her ears. He wants to slap her. She holds Hops between her legs, and she says, "Call me Hops, Michael." She jumps, flings herself down, coughing, croaking. He wants to kick her silly. She just comes off the refrigerator and onto the floor into a hapless spill.

"What's the word for you?" Ruth, ex-wife to Coin and mother of Nadine, says.

Coin's come with his one question. What's up with their daughter?

At the door Ruth said, "Your baby's having a baby. Rejoice."

This woman is two years older than Coin, and she sits here across from him in Levi's and cowboy boots, her hair blunt and pugnacious, saying, "Earnest," and nailing the heel of one boot to the toe of the other one.

Earnest? Coin thinks.

"To a fault," Ruth says. "It's the word for you, Coin. Earnest to a fault." She's taking her boots off.

Her boy comes in and whispers to her. She says back to the boy, "Ask him."

The boy is seven. His name is Samuel. He belongs to Ruth and the man she is living with. Samuel says to Coin, "Do you know what time it is in L.A.?"

Coin raises his clueless hands.

"Four," Samuel says.

"A.M. or P.M.?" Coin says.

Samuel pulls Ruth to him and whispers to her. She whispers back. The boy comes up to Coin and says, "It's apples and oranges, Coin."

It is, Coin thinks. He says, "It's apples and oranges," and gets up to leave.

Ruth walks him out.

He says, "The two of us, me and Nadine—we don't talk. You do, don't you? You and Nadine? Is it Michael—is there a problem with Michael?"

Ruth, angled into the doorframe, says, "Your daughter is

acting like this is not the twentieth century. She's talking like she is someone's grandmother. You're her father, Coin, and she wants you to tell her what to do. Only you can't. She's your baby, has always been your baby. Baby your baby, Coin."

Samuel, thigh-deep in Ruth's cowboy boots and red-faced, is coming down the hall in chunky jerks. He is joggle-eyed and is saying, "You're a good man, Coin."

Three A.M., and Coin gets a phone call from Nadine. She is in Massachusetts and has been to The Church of the Living God, where she did sob sob sob for a reverend. She asked him questions point-blank and put him in tears.

"The issue is not this, and the issue is not that," she says. She tells Coin the issue isn't the world, and it isn't what she wants. The issue is we are all part of God.

Coin sees her in the Sculpture Garden, circling Picasso's *She-Goat*, taking her poky steps. She is in her plum-colored coat, and the sunlight is on her. She has a part in her hair he has never seen before. Her hands are deep in her pockets, and the red enamel heart marks her heart.

At what point will her mass double and send her, shoe over shoe, onto her head?

He says, "The issue is, exactly where are you?"

"No, Coin," she says. "The issue is not where am I. The issue is where am I going."

Nadine tells him she will call wherever it is.

What is the word for Nadine up here on the refrigerator, Hops between her legs, the two of them hunkered into some kind of last rite for the dead? What can Coin do for Nadine sitting here, what can he do for his daughter, who is mad enough to spit?

The Glue That Binds Us

Mornings, I wake up, and glumness mugs me before my feet hit the floor. In a fit, some spoilsport goaty god has come down hard on me. I'm Colfisch. The gods? They interfere, *a tort et a travers*, without rhyme or reason. I tiptoe along walls from corner to corner and hope to avoid the ax.

This particular day? The sky is teal, and the sun is a yellow coin. We're outside at Benjamin Gust's condo in Park City, Utah, forty-five minutes up Parley's Canyon from Salt Lake City, on a hardwood patio under umbrellas that are cranked against the heat. Gloria and I have come back to Utah on a visit. Gust's staying in the condo while we use his house in Salt Lake. Old friends have come up for the day, and some of Gust's neighbors have dropped in. The umbrellas are pied green and yellow, and there is a lot of latticework around. Clay pots filled with red and white geraniums sit on the tables.

My heart's one sound is a two-beat *thud-hud*. Open my collar and listen. Hear it?

Gloria's at another table, sitting with Zinnia Smith and Gust. I can tell by the way she's acting she's talking about the money. Yesterday, out of the blue, a man walks up and gives her eleven hundred dollars.

Here's my theory, my idea of what the gods are up to, what they're telling me. I'm too full of myself. I'm not a thanker, not an I'm-sorryer. I've rubbed a god the wrong way. I've ticked him off. I know corporate law, and the result is money rolls in. Now, one-hundred-dollar bills from heaven are being shoved down my throat.

A woman across from me sips lemonade and says to the woman sitting next to her, "It's hard on shoes." *It*, I've picked up, is Oregon. The state of Oregon is hard on shoes.

"It ruins them," I say, trying to join in.

They slant their eyes at me. *Wiseass*, they think.

I raise my lemonade to them.

The woman who spoke first says, "It starts at the stitching."

"Fresh drinks?" I say, getting up.

They squint at me. Whatever happened to *No, but thank you*?

Gloria is untying a ribbon from Zinnia's hair, winding it around her own finger. Gust asks for the ribbon. I stop and say, "Nice to see you all." Zinnia's hair is bronze. She says, "Having fun?" She puts little quotes around *having fun?*

"I'll live," I say.

Gloria has given Gust the ribbon and is fiddling with Zinnia's blouse. She twists its tails into a knot.

Women handle each other. Men don't—do they?

What hits me hard when I pour a fresh drink is that I want the floor. I've got an announcement to make. Me, Colfisch, I want to say that Gloria no longer likes me. She may not even love me.

I feel unruly, and I want to talk. Her not liking me is a fact. We're not kids, not teenagers, not twenty-year-olds, and I'm not stupid. We're in our fifties, and we've left billing and cooing behind. Love isn't the question. What matters is liking. Liking counts. Love can't save you. What goes wrong is wives come to dislike husbands, and husbands come to dislike wives. Reciprocity. I know facts, and I'm familiar with emotions. I know the law. I've seen what you haven't. Me, Colfisch, I'm nobody's fool. Men, women. Women, men. Hear the beat? With me, it's a *thud-hud*.

Yahweh, overfed and world-weary, grows testy, calls in a few minor gods so his words will be heard, and says, "Let's break the rules, like pots."

So, a few days ago, on a Monday, a man comes up to Gloria on a downtown Salt Lake City street and hands her eleven one-hundred-dollar bills. The story makes the *Tribune*, only the reporter bungles the facts. He says one thousand dollars. It was *eleven* hundred, *eleven* one-hundred-dollar bills. The man did not say, as the paper says he did, "God wants you to have this." He said, "Greetings from your Heavenly Father and your Heavenly Mother, who want you to have this money in order that you shall never want again." If you'd heard him, Gloria claims, you would not have forgotten the exact words.

When she sat me down to tell me what happened, she said, "The young man said, 'Greetings.' Greetings, like he was from another planet." He said Heavenly Father and Heavenly Mother, not god. "How did they get it wrong?" she said, and she studied me like I had something up my sleeve. Her look was hard enough to make me wonder if I was part of some plot.

Like I say, the gods interfere. Sure, we invite them. We wear hair shirts, smudge ash across our foreheads. We cry, *For pity! For pity!* and sing, *De Profundis*. We file our grievances.

Gloria sat me down and said, "I was not waiting for a bus. I was ten feet from the bus stop. Gust was coming to get me." She read from the *Tribune*, from "Riding the UTA Pays Off." It said, *A San Diego, California, woman received a pleasant surprise while she was waiting for a UTA bus at Main and South Temple. Gloria Colfisch was approached by a young well-dressed man who gave her one thousand dollars and said, "God wants you to have this."*

"Approached," Gloria said, and she was angry. There was air caught inside her. Her eyes bulged.

I told her it was only a newspaper and what did she expect.

"They spoiled it," she said. "Approached is sleazy. It wasn't sleazy."

The man was handsome. He wore a blue suit, a vest, a white shirt and a tie he'd loosened at the collar. Gloria said to me, "Colfisch, he could have been our son, except he had no facial hair. He was our boy before our boy's beard." She yanked out a photo of our son and tried to cover up his beard.

I stood and held my body so she saw that I understand how strange a place the world is.

Exactly one week later, on a Monday, I am standing on Main and South Temple, ten feet from the bus stop, right where Gloria was when the man who looks like our son minus a beard gave her the eleven one-hundred-dollar bills. It's noon. I am thinking that Gust is someone Gloria does not dislike. Gust, she says, has a kid in him he hasn't killed off.

Implication is, of course, that I've bumped off the kid in me. I've knuckled under. I'm a windbag, which is a thing Gloria herself has called me. My motto is *est modus in rebus*. There is a proper measure in all things.

Silly Latin leaps from me. Not from Gust.

Gust sells used cars. You see him on TV. He's up on a ladder wielding a bullhorn and declaring that Gust's Cars, all five locations, will be open Labor Day. He climbs the steps, and, halfway up, the bullhorn squawking like Gust has wrung its neck, he swings it to his mouth and says, "Sales must go up up up." He keeps climbing. At the top, he says, "Our inventory is sky high." The bullhorn screeches. He pulls sparkling cardboard dollar signs out of his pockets, tosses them in the air, and says, "Prices are coming down down down."

It's all in fun. His bad taste is good taste. Everyone likes him. Okay, *I* like Gust.

Gloria spends her days with him, and I walk around like a sorehead. I say I don't mind. I've got people to see. Gust is divorced, and his children are gone. He needs company.

The problem is not Gust. It's not the eleven one-hundred-dollar bills. Something I can put into words is that what's gone wrong is like a junky heartbeat. My pulse says, *Men, women. Women, men. Husbands, wives. Me, Gloria. Gloria, me. Colf-fisch. Like, dislike.*

Could be it's Salt Lake City. Having gotten out, having packed bags and things and made it to San Diego, I'm asking myself, What are we doing back, even for two weeks? I'm here on Main and South Temple with my hands in my pockets, and over my shoulder, on top of the Mormon temple, is a gold angel blowing a long horn. They say he'll trumpet in the second coming of Christ. His first blast will undo the wicked, and his second will raise the righteous dead. To my left, thirty feet above the traffic, is a statue of Brigham Young, the Mormon who led them to Utah. He's extending one hand and leaning on a cane, saying, "This is the place." The joke around here used to be he was pointing to a bank. The Mormons are a rich bunch. Corporate America does its business here.

Gloria was waiting for Gust at twelve-thirty. I came at eleven, and it's now one. Buses come and go. I've brought along a picture of our son minus his beard.

At one-thirty I give up and head for Lamb's restaurant two blocks down Main. I find a booth in the back, order lunch, and think about Gloria not liking me. No one's arguing I'm pretty at fifty-five. My belly's slid beyond my chest, and my legs are wobbly. The hair all over my body is blacker. My arms are spotted, here and there pigment loss, and there are blotches on my stomach that look like coffee stains. Ugly stuff. Ointment would help, but I'm not up for a dermatologist. We age, and the body expands here, shrivels up somewhere else. Parts pucker, wrinkle. What is it they say? We taper off. Joy ebbs. Our moons wane more than they wax.

And what does it mean to be a lawyer? Not much. Early retirement. Land to live off. I'm not high-minded, and I don't read, would rather see a spy movie than some foreign film. I'm a sports man. I'll admit I watch more than I play, but I put in some golf. My swing's not bad.

Sex? Have I ever had enough equipment? No one's complained, and Colfisch's fifty-five-year-old tool manages, can get itself up and beyond horizontal. Still, I'm fat, and I wouldn't want me on me.

Is Gloria suffering Colfisch? Biding her time? Living off fantasies of life without the old fart?

Gloria. Me. Gust.

Am I being traded in?

Here in Lamb's, in the booth in front of mine, is a young man who could be our son. From one angle, he's our boy. I get up and say, "Excuse me." He jumps. He was reading the paper, and I surprised him. "Forgive me," I say. I'm polite, let him settle himself. I say, "Can we talk?"

He can't place me, but is thinking I could be important. Somehow I might add up to money. My suit cost nine hundred, and my hair is trimmed three times a week even on vacations. He says, "Certainly." He moves to get up, reaching out to shake my hand, saying, "Please. Have a seat." He's not as sure about me as he would like to be. Who knows who is crazy? I hold his hand a beat too long, then sit across from him. He says, "You have me at the disadvantage. I don't remember your name." He folds his newspaper and puts it aside.

"We've not met," I say.

Now his eyes mix it up. They're pinballs. He knows all the nuts are not in the bin.

I say, "My name is Colfisch."

A waitress walks over and says, "Will you be eating here?"

"If this gentleman will let me buy his lunch," I say.

He protests, and I insist. I win. I order juice, and he asks for more coffee.

I say to him, "One week ago, on a Monday like today, a young man comes up to my wife and gives her eleven one-hundred-dollar bills. She is on South Temple, and he hands her eleven hundred dollars. He looks like our son, only our son has grown a beard, and the man didn't have facial hair. He is neatly dressed and clean. Not a bum, my wife says. From behind, from where I was sitting, when you tilt your head, you look like our son." He rubs his forehead, squinting at me like I've walked out of swamp. I say, "Maybe you saw the article in the paper." He looks at the *Tribune*. "On Wednesday," I say.

He says, "Sir, my name is Singer, and I'm from New Jersey. Aaron Singer." He lifts his hand to shake mine again, realizes that's dumb and drops it hard enough to rattle our dishes. He rips at a muffin and says, "I've been in Utah five years, praying each day to get out, and I didn't give your wife eleven hundred dollars."

I say, "I didn't think you did."

He gives me a look that says, *So?*

"You're smart. I can see that," I say. "I'm not a dummy. I'm smart, too. I'm a lawyer, and I can't figure this out. This guy tells my wife that her Heavenly Father and her Heavenly Mother want her to have the money. His words are *in order that you will never want again.* My wife quotes him. There are good reasons, and then there are real reasons. You know what I mean. I can see you know what I mean. Tell me, why do you think he gave her the money? Your guess, what is your guess?"

He says, "You don't need money."

"We're stinking rich," I say. "Five cars. Two of us, and five cars. A home in Tahoe. We live in San Diego. Why eleven one-hundred-dollar bills? Why not a thousand bucks? Why Gloria? Why not the poor?"

Singer says, "My guess?"

"Your guess." I show him the picture I have of our son, try to turn it so Singer will see himself if I can get the angle right.

He says, "Here's what I think." He works out his guess on a linen napkin. Using a Bic, he draws boxes and labels them. He makes arrows that connect small boxes and big boxes, linking money from here to there. It's business, simple and financial. He says, "It's as American as baseball. The guy who looks like your son was somebody's hand. He passes it out. That's all."

"And Gloria?"

"Random. Your mind-set is contracts, precedents. You want guides. You need justification. Party of the first part, party of the second part, rights as agreed upon. Think chaos, Colfisch."

"*A propos de rien.*"

"What?"

"Apropos of nothing."

"No rhyme or reason."

We leave together and walk up Main toward Brigham Young. I can't let it drop. I'm edgy. I say, "You're kidding me."

"Not me," Singer says. In the sunlight, he comes across flat as a bad snapshot.

"Why not sock it away? It's stupid, but why not bury it in tin cans? Hide it in a mattress? Find a write-off?"

"No fun," he says.

"Fun?"

"Fun, Colfisch," Singer says.

At South Temple, he says, "Colfisch, what are two Jews doing in Salt Lake City, Utah?"

Brigham Young is pointing at us. I hear the first blast of the angel's horn above the traffic.

Inside I'm snarling. I've got the Cubs on cable when Gloria comes out of the bedroom wearing a sundress. Her shoulders are tan. In the time we've been here, she's filled Gust's closets with new clothes. They shop together. They go to malls. She's added pottery to his end tables.

"Can't you come?" she says, and she twirls, really gets up on her toes and goes around and around. "Get yourself out of the dumps," she says. She and Gust are going to a car show then to dinner.

I say, "I don't mind the dumps," and I hold up a yellow legal pad as if to say, *Can't you see when a man's busy as hell?* At the top of the pad I've written, WHAT ARE TWO JEWS DOING IN SALT LAKE CITY, UTAH?

Gloria lowers the sound on the TV. "Colfisch," she says, "you're coming apart."

I write *Colfisch Colfisch Colfisch* and feel sour.

"Come with us," she says, walking toward the window, listening for Gust's honk. She closes the blinds against the sun. She shifts cut-glass figurines and asks about the Cubs.

I say, "Colfisch is coming apart." I've written it on my pad. To it, I add, *At the seams*, and I think, *Who'll pick up the pieces?* I write out, *Utah is a state that is hard on Colfisches.*

"I feel springy," Gloria says, and she holds her dress out like a girl at her first recital. She bounces toward me, saying, "Not Springy springy, like the time of year. But springy, like I have my wits about me and yet I'm drunk with joy."

What I see is her fist around the eleven one-hundred-dollar bills the day she told me the paper got all the facts wrong.

On my pad, I write, *Springy*.

Gust honks, and Gloria says, "Meet us for dinner?"

I wiggle-waggle the legal pad at her.

"Seven o'clock, if you change your mind," she says.

I get up and thank her. We walk out to Gust's BMW, and they wave as they drive off.

What have I done? Sent my wife on a date?

The Cubs are losing, and there's nothing to drink in the house. Gust is a Mormon. For that matter, Gloria is something of a Mormon.

I sit on Gust's couch and write on my pad, *Pigheaded*. Pigheaded is what I don't want to be, is what I can be, and am too often. I add *Bellyacher* to *Pigheaded*. A Pigheaded Bellyacher. God, I am what I don't want to be. Wimps, queers, politicians—they bellyache. The army taught me not to. The army said, Face up. I write, *FACE UP.* All caps.

A Met drives a Cub pitch into the bleachers, and the center fielder slumps like a hawk has just unloaded on him. In the stands, two men with rainbow hairdos have stretched out a banner that says, JOHN 3:16. You've seen it, haven't you? At the Masters behind a golfer teeing up, during the NBA playoffs, between goal posts at football games. I write John 3:16 on my pad and go hunt for a bible. All I can find is a Mormon one.

John 3:16 says, "For God so loved the world, that he gave his only begotten Son, that whosoever believeth in him should not perish, but have everlasting life." I copy it down.

Here's what I have:

WHAT ARE TWO JEWS DOING IN SALT LAKE CITY, UTAH?
Colfisch Colfisch Colfisch
Colfisch is coming apart at the seams.
Utah is a state that is hard on Colfisches
Springy
Pigheaded Bellyacher
FACE UP

John 3:16: For God so loved the world, that he gave his only begotten Son, that whosoever believeth in him should not perish, but have everlasting life.

I add *AGONY,* all caps, which I feel in my bones.

The question is, Should I pack my bags and steal away in the night like a good sport?

On my knees, head denting the couch, I put my hand on the back of my neck and pretend it is Gloria's hand. If it were hers, if I glanced up now and saw her here, I'd tell her what I know about springy, how I've lost it.

What I'd say, what I'd be doing is trying to keep our balance on a lake of ice.

The phone rings.

I scuttle around the couch on my knees and pick it up. It's Zinnia. She says, "Gloria?"

I say, "No." I'm silently crying.

"It's past midnight," Zinnia says.

I'm writing on my legal pad, at the top of a new page, *WHAT IS THE GLUE THAT BINDS US?*

Zinnia says, "Is she with Benjamin?"

"Dinner," I say. "A car show, then dinner." Under *WHAT IS THE GLUE THAT BINDS US?* I put, *Love of:*

"Tell her I called," Zinnia says.

"Will do."

Next morning I'm up and gone before Gloria leaves with Gust. My legal pad is under my arm. To it, I've added the evidence I have that Gloria no longer likes me. There is the look in her eye and the air in the rooms we occupy. There is the way she dodges me.

A short piece in the local section of yesterday's *Tribune* said a woman named Christiensen was handed five one-hundred-dollar bills by a young man while she was waiting for a bus at 1300 East and Fort Union Boulevard. He didn't talk to her. Attached to the money was a note that said, *Hi. Your Heavenly*

Father and your Heavenly Mother want you to have this, as you will never need money again.

At Lamb's, I sit in the booth Singer sat in and order what I remember him having. My legal pad is next to my plate. I've paperclipped the picture of our son to it, the one of him without his beard.

What's been done to me has been done without justification, and I've come to argue my case. I'm here in my defense. *Se defendendo.*

To Singer's face, I'll say, *The gods too are under contract. Willy-nilly doesn't cut it.*

Singer doesn't show for breakfast.

I'm patient. I double-check my facts. *Life,* I'll say, *is a legal matter.*

No Singer for lunch.

There is something shady about Singer, as if he keeps a dagger on his body.

I scribble a beard on the photo of my son, then read him my evidence. I ask him what he'd write under WHAT IS THE GLUE THAT BINDS US? *Love of:*

I say, "Answer me."

A waitress steps over and says, "Did you say something?"

"Coffee," I say.

My newly bearded son grins at me.

At two I'm headed north on Main. Our son has kept himself tight-lipped, and Singer did not show. I'm asking the wrong questions of the wrong man in the wrong place. I pass a bum who looks like Singer in rags. He wears a sign that says, DON'T TOUCH ME MY ARMS COME OFF. He gives me a flyer and says, "May the wind always be at your back." The flyer tells me where I can get running shoes for a 30 percent discount.

The Mormons' gold angel stands in a neon-blue sky and toots his horn. I flip back a page on my legal pad and write, THIS IS A HOAX; flip the next page and write, THIS IS NOT A HOAX. I'll flip and write until I run out of pages.

What's to lose? Appointments with the gods cannot be postponed. They announce. We cheer. One does not plea bargain with them. There are no lighter sentences. Their will be done. So, I join Gust and Gloria, go with them to a benefit for a Ronald McDonald House the night before Gloria and I are to leave Salt Lake.

We're in black tie, and Gloria is in grey. Two city blocks around the Hotel Utah have been roped off, and there is a band in a gazebo playing marches. Women are auctioning quilts. I pay six hundred for a Pennsylvania Dutch design. Gloria says, "Now you re-donate it."

Tonight I'm a joiner. I admire my quilt, then I get up on a stage and talk fast. I'm gibbering, and it's pleasing people, like this is a hoedown. I can hear them: *Hey, Colfisch is a fun guy.* A man who looks like the Jack of Diamonds buys my quilt. Gust pays a thousand for an antique organ pump, and I bid on a speedboat. Madame Chekhovsky, her damp hands on my ears, her nose swung up toward the heavens, prophesies. She says, "Your heart is big. It beats like the Mississippi. This day, you will write out a check for two thousand dollars, and you will give it to—" She raises one finger and tilts her head. "To," she says, "to the Ronald McDonald House." I'm already reaching for my checkbook and a pen.

Gloria leads me and Gust into a courtyard, and Gust says, "Tic-tac-toe." The game's at our feet. Nine boxes make up an eight-foot square. The wood is oak. A poster says a master craftsman handmade each box.

"Here," Gust says, and he is handing me a bean bag. He's pinned a fifty-dollar bill to one he's holding and is leaning over to toss it into one of the boxes. He says, "I'm X's," and loops his bag toward the center box.

I rubberband a fifty to my bag and drop it in a box.

"Got you," he says.

I've screwed up the first move, forgot what eight-year-olds know, and Gust wins. I have to match the total amount we've put in the boxes.

We eat walking around, and Gust guides us to a poetry reading. The poet is a young man from India who reads only in his own language. He stands stiffly, as if he was raised in a box. People come in, listen, then leave. We stay half an hour. Gloria told me Gust is writing poetry, and she has read most of it. It makes her cry.

Ballroom dancing begins at nine, and I learn that Gust and Gloria have been taking lessons. They've paid and gone to a studio. I don't dance.

We enter the hall as music begins. "Ach du lieber Augustin," Gust says.

"Try it?" Gloria says to me.

I say, "You go."

Gust says, "If you can walk, you can dance."

"Nursery rhymes," I say.

Gloria winks at me and takes Gust's hand. They fit, Gloria and Gust. She's the height he needs, and when they pick up the beat he sheds whatever it is that makes him Gust. His arms flash, cut angles as flawless as shark fins. His right hand was born to the spot it finds between her shoulders and waist, and her left hand seeks his neck. He carries his weight. She carries hers. He steps, and she replies. It's like a great quarrel.

A tango begins. I go outside, where I sit on a retaining wall that holds a fountain and flowers. The poet we listened to is talking to a group of people nearby. He laughs, *hat hat hat.* The end of a joke. He comes over and studies the fountain. It puzzles him. Over his shoulder, in the blue-black sky, is the angel on top of the Mormon temple lighted from underneath. The poet stands by me like a guest waiting to be announced.

I say, "Hello."

"May I?" he says and sits too close. Our knees touch.

I slide away, saying, "I've been trying to name the flowers. But I don't know flowers. I don't know what they are. Something tells me poets can name all the flowers."

He lights a cigarette and without looking at the flowers says, "Daffodils, mums, daisies, roses." He drops smoke from his mouth, then says, "Touch-me-nots, marigolds, cyclamen. Hibiscus."

First Singer, now a poet from India. Is there a sign on me that says KID THIS MAN / PUT HIM ON / HE LOVES IT?

"Am I in the ballpark?" he says.

I say, "Out in left field."

He gives me, *hat hat hat,* then says, "My name is Charanjit Singh, and I am living in Tucson, Arizona, where it is the desert I love. It dries out my poems." His dark eyes follow a woman who is coaxing a man toward the ballroom.

I say, "Your poems are dry?"

"Your American women," he says, "they wear hairdos like tumbleweeds." He holds his cigarette away from us. His hand is a rodent's foot.

I get up, saying, "I think I'll locate my wife."

Singh bends over until the top of his head almost touches his feet. From down under, he says, "Kids say the damnedest things."

Years ago, Gust and I were in a pickup basketball game at the Deseret Gym, and he caught me with an elbow. I nailed him, one shot, and he went down. I broke his jaw. He sat in the emergency room, no shirt on, not as fat as he is now, but red welts all over his body. He looked like he'd been hit with strawberries. He gets the welts when he's nervous. You can see them on his neck.

Inside, Gloria is talking to the governor, and Gust is dancing with Zinnia. The Blue Danube. Zinnia's husband is some kind of aide to the governor. What I remember most about him is that he mispronounces words.

Gloria sees me and says, "Colfisch."

I say hello to the governor and ask him about the drought. He shrugs. "If I'd've planned for drought, we'd have had floods," he says.

Everyone takes on looks that say FATE, all caps.

Gloria and I sit on Gust's patio, in the dark, under an awning that runs the length of the back of the house, me in my tux, Gloria in grey. Driving us back, Gust tried to talk us into staying another week. "What obligations do you have?" he said. "You haven't seen the lake. Saltair is back in business, and some sculptor built a monument out on the Salt Flats, a shaft of cement two hundred feet high with billiard balls on top of it."

"Got to get back," I said.

"What's in San Diego you haven't done?" he said. "Stay six weeks, a year. Stick around till Christmas. We'll swap gifts. Antique cars."

One thing that isn't in San Diego is some nut running around giving women one-hundred-dollar bills.

Gust followed us to the door. He said, "I'll be here before you leave."

Gloria said, "It's your house, Ben. Stay here tonight." She was tired.

"I'll be here early," he said.

Gloria said, "We'll have breakfast."

Now Gloria and I sit on his lounge chairs, and I count his wind chimes. There are wooden ones, steel ones, ceramic ones that clank. One set is made up of cylinders. Where does a man like Gust buy them? And why?

Gloria says, "Last night, when Gust brought me home, he asked me to sit in the car for a minute." She sips a Coke I got her.

I think, *Necking?*

She says, "He asked me to pray with him."

"To pray with him?"

"He and Zinnia are sleeping together," she says.

I can see Zinnia's bronze hair on a pillow and her fingers putting quote marks around *sleeping together*. Her husband is a Mormon bishop.

I say, "He wanted to pray about screwing around?"

"Well," she says, "it's bad. I tried to lighten it up. I said, 'I don't pray. I wring my hands.'"

"How?" I say. "On your knees?"

"Just sitting in the car."

"Did you?"

"He did."

"He prayed in front of you?"

"It was no big thing," she says.

I think about Charanjit Singh and how squeezed-in he was. He is not my idea of a poet. Gust is not my idea of a man.

Gloria says, "Colfisch, is this it?"

It? I think.

She says, "Do we end up pitiful, all of us?"

My heart does its *thud-bud*, and out of the corner of my eye I see Gloria looking up as if she can see through the awning that something from outer space is about to land. I want to yell *No!* but can't get air. I stumble over to a wind chime and try out a tune.

"Coming back is a possibility," she says, and she has gotten up and put an arm around me. "Reincarnation," she says. "I think that poet was writing about coming back. Who is the woman who is claiming she remembers living before as different things and people?"

I say, "A thousand people say that."

"No. She's famous. A movie star."

"Makes it worse."

"I'd like to come back as you," Gloria says, and she pulls me toward the house and into the kitchen. She says, "Civility. A sense of who you are. You have these things, Colfisch."

I could walk on water.

She says, "Don't you think it means something, the seven chakras of the body, the seven colors of the rainbow, the seven musical notes?"

Singer comes to mind, a wicked man who has simplified life, who could simplify ours. I say, "Fun."

Gloria says, "Fun?"

"Why not?" I say. "Got a better answer? Heard of anything better from the gods?"

Out of her purse, she pulls out the eleven one-hundred-dollar bills and says, "We leave tonight."

"Gust?" I say.

"Screw Gust," she says.

"Zinnia is," I say.

We're bumping into each other and knocking things over in Gust's house.

"Vegas," she says.

I could scale rock cliffs. *Resurgam.*

She says, "Why wait for Vegas? Wendover's two hours away. Maybe we can get lost in Ne-vah-dah."

I say, "You've got more than a little of the devil in you."

"And you don't?" she says.

We're packed by three A.M., and I'm vacuuming when the phone rings. Gloria's drying sheets we've washed. The phone is Zinnia, whispering. "Gloria?" she says. I get Gloria. I empty waste baskets and straighten out throw pillows. I fold the sheets, put them in cupboards, and load up the car.

By five we're headed west, Gloria driving, me letting Salt Lake City leak from my bones. Gloria wrote Gust a note and stuck it to the front door. It said, *Eleven hundred dollars burning a hole in my purse. Wendover calling us. See you next time and think about coming to San Diego.*

She says to me, "Zinnia's a mess."

I say, "What'd you tell her?"

"To run off with Gust."

"Will she?"

Gloria looks at me in the dark car and says, "You don't know what it is to be a Mormon."

"Do you?"

She says, "You don't think you can be a god."

"And you do?"

"Mormons do."

"Mormons can be God?"

"A god. And Gust thinks so. He's a priesthood holder."

We're past the lake, and the Salt Flats stretch out in the grey morning light like a linen table cloth. One more nudge from one more malcontented god and I can see myself hotfooting it across the flats to the blue mountains at the edge of the earth. Up ahead, the monument the sculptor built, the one Gust told us about, rises out of the whiteness. The morning sun has turned it pink, and no matter how delicate you want to be you have to admit it looks like a giant's dick poking into the earth. It's got balls.

Wendover is less than twenty miles away, and we're flying when we pass the monument. Now I count seven huge balls on top. They're numbered and striped.

Gloria says, "Someone ought to lasso that and pull it down."

There is probably twice as much of it in the ground as there is showing.

Just before we top a small rise, I turn around and see the Salt Flats spread out endlessly. I see the sculptor in his hometown in Finland or Sweden, wherever it is. He's drinking old-world beer from an ornate stein and resting his elbows on a wooden table, telling anyone who will listen how he went to the U S of A and put the entire state of Utah on.

Let Me Tell You What Ward DiPino Tells Me at Work

Ward DiPino roars in, slugs open the door. Says, "You take hard American cash?" He's spilled a hatful of silver dollars on the counter and is stacking them up.

I'm at the 7-Eleven doing my week of graveyards. It's after one A.M. DiPino's Cadillac simmers in a slot out front.

The dollars are a foot high and leaning. He aligns them with a frisky left hand and pushes his hat back off his head. It's a regulation, forest-green Boy Scout leader's hat, rivet-holed and stiff-brimmed as a plate. It ends up between DiPino's shoulders, held there by a cord that cuts into his neck. DiPino studies the dollars, then me. His eyes zig like tiny sailboats. We know each other from around the corner at Johnny Pocco's Ringside Gym, Las Vegas's Home of World Champions. He says to me, "Poppy."

I set my hands like I've got training mitts on, and I say, "Left."

Smack, DiPino's left stings my palm.

I say, "Right."

It's then I see his right hand is wrapped in a bloody towel. It comes up and thuds against my left.

I say, "Left."

Smack.

"Left."

Smack.

"Right."

Let Me Tell You What Ward DiPino Tells Me at Work 153

Thud.

DiPino's footwork is skip-rope rococo.

Orin, Mary, and Hatch, three geriatrics who spend their worst hours in here, have stopped pumping quarters into the video poker machines. Mary is trying to disappear up one of the aisles, and Hatch acts seasick. Orin nabs a magazine and starts flapjacking its pages. Walking backwards, one hand feeling behind him for trouble, Hatch knocks over a stool. Mary hooks Orin's suspenders, pulls him in close, and bows her head.

DiPino creeps over. Mary, black orthopedic pumps under her wing, was holding four clubs to a flush and the dream of two hundred and fifty dollars in quarters. DiPino whumps down on the arm of her machine and up pops the ten of diamonds. He hands her her cup of quarters and says to the three of them, "Scoot."

They blink and walk into each other, knock around like pool balls. I can picture the fools slapsticking themselves into a pile of arms and legs.

"Scoot," DiPino says and flicks them away, saying, "I'm a rascal." A fish lure dangles from one ear.

The geriatrics, their collective thought is, Drugs. What they've only seen in movies is about to come true.

DiPino says, "Scoot. Scamper. You know, scamper, to run nimbly and playfully about. In this case to run nimbly and playfully out the door."

Hatch, eyes rolled up, squeaks past, and Orin abandons his Big Gulp and a knit tie. DiPino holds the door for Mary. He's charmed her.

He says, "Arrrrgh."

DiPino spars big time, and he's been on some million-dollar cards at Caesar's, the prelim's subprelim. I jump some rope at Johnny Pocco's, and I lift a little. DiPino's added meaning to my shadowboxing and helped me put together some hand-to-eye workouts. His basic living is dealing twenty-one downtown at the Golden Nugget. The busted up hand will put a stop to that.

Orin, Mary, and Hatch are out in the parking lot under

a streetlight near the gasoline pumps, scratching their heads and butts, rubbernecking. DiPino puts a case of Bud on the counter, hops and skips away, comes back, and clanks down two cold ones he's gotten from the cooler. His t-shirt is black and rolled up at the sleeves. It says, NO DICE on the front.

He says, "Kools?"

I get them.

"How much?" he says, and he points at the beer and cigarettes. He takes a lighter from a display, says, "And this?" and slides it into his pocket.

I twist the lids off the beer and punch in the prices.

He pinches a silver dollar off the top of his stack and bites it, then a second one, and a third. Smoke leaks from his mouth. I tell him what he owes, and he pays me in silver. He says, "Honest money."

He's barefoot, has big toes, like hard fruit has sprung from his feet. His eyes continue to zig and tack, and the fish lure swings. He sees me eyeballing his bloody hand and says, "Not to worry." The capacity of my heart is about to be tested. DiPino pokes out his cigarette and gives me his left hand. We shake faglike, fingers clamped to fingers, and he dips in his knees, offers up a girly curtsy. Says, "Ain't I the daintiest?" He whips his bloody hand around so fast the towel unwraps, and blood splatters on the walls and the floor and the front windows. "Ain't I the cat's meow, the cream of the crop, an ace." His knuckles are crushed. He lights another Kool one-handed, gulps another beer. Says, "Drink up."

My first beer's untouched, so I down it, and I say, "One on me?" My eyes are watering.

DiPino's face flies wide open, and I head for the cooler. He tags along behind me, making noises you'd think only a rocking chair could make. He says, "I'm indomitable." He's in the way when I reach for two more Buds. He says, "Unconquerable. Incapable of being vanquished." He unfurls six feet of arm, of scalloped bicep and lanky tendon, of forearm thick as tension-bridge cable, of an arrogant bloody fist. He says, "My indomitableness is as long as my reach."

Let Me Tell You What Ward DiPino Tells Me at Work   155

He snags a bag of chips on our way back to the counter, and we clink our beers together, me on my side and him on his. He says, "Ring up the cost. I'm paying. They say there ain't no free lunch, and I'm God's living proof." He hands me silver. Says, "Arrrrgh," and pretends to hang something in the air. He says, "Punching bag," and he outlines its shape for me to see. His cigarette sputters, his bare cleat-hard feet pit and pat, and he punches the bag, jackhammer stuff. If air could suffer, it would.

He is boxing and jabbering, saying, "I get inside you when I fight. I punch from in there, and I don't mean in close. I don't mean I'm on top of you. What I'm saying is I'm destroying your body, your liver, your stomach. I'm *in*side you. Hooks. Uppercuts. I kill you from in there."

He stops, drops his hands to his sides, and kind of rolls them up like he's got hold of weights. The right one is dripping blood. Ash falls to the linoleum, and he swallows the butt. Chases it with beer. Lights another Kool.

He says, "I tell you this so you'll know what it takes to put my tail between my legs." He feints, bobs, jabs.

A kid on a skateboard appears in the door. He flicks a foot to the side of the board, and it springs into his hands. He spins the board like a football. DiPino spits beer. Says, "Beat it. Men only here, and we're talking."

The kid is deaf or ignorant. He doesn't move. His black hair's a monkey's cap.

DiPino flips him a silver dollar. Says, "Buy your shit elsewhere."

The kid is on the skateboard in reverse, his foot smacking the blacktop, both eyes pinned to us. He U-turns, hits the parking lot like a maniac trout, and is sucked into the night.

DiPino says, "Music."

I show him the tape rack. Everything's cheap, the best of some burned-out old rock star, so-and-so's greatest hits, pop, easy listening, a little country western, and enough gospel.

He takes western and is unsealing the tape and headed for his Cadillac, tossing me silver dollars, saying, "Ring it up." He climbs into his backseat and emerges with a boom box, which he hefts to a shoulder, and I hear the music before he's inside. Some man is stomping on some woman's heart. He plays it hard. I've twisted the caps off two more beers.

DiPino lights a Kool from the one he's about to stub out. The music sits on the counter, twang twang twang. DiPino's bloody hand floats near his chin. He makes a fist, lets it go. He shudders. You'd think he'd just eaten unplucked chicken.

I'm thinking, What can I swap here? What can I do to get this man on my side? He's about to unload on someone. He needs to see we're from the same side of the tracks. We're peas in a pod. We need a trade, straight across, even-Steven. Life for life. My story for his. You don't hurt the ones you tell your secrets to. I say, "Want to hear about my lady and her dogs?"

He says, "Is it ugly?"

"It's ugly," I say.

"Shoot," he says.

I tell him about the married lady I see, fill him in. Jane and me, we met when I was doing some cut work for two middle weights at Caesar's. I let DiPino know how she's rich and gets us into opening night any show on the strip and into jai-alai. You name it, and she can manage tickets, best seat in whatever house. Her connections are her husband's. Tonight, before I come to work, she has me over to dinner. Her hair is done-up, hangs like a garden. Their place is three acres in El Cortez Circle. Everything looks Spanish. She's got German Shepherds to protect her. The dogs cost more than most cars and come from the Black Forest in Germany. They're bigger than polar bears and low-slung. Their muzzles are dark as beards.

Her husband's gone, and the dinner is catered, me and the lady sitting across a linen tablecloth, her looking like we're going to the White House. Candles. Her dress is checkered, black and white, and its collar is layered like a flower bud's petals. Her lips—they're moonbeams. Each earring is a white pearl the shape of a tear.

I say to DiPino, "I'm wearing a neighbor's tie and the pants

I've got on." Me and DiPino, we both look at my spat-on tired-out chinos.

"Ain't it the truth," he says.

I stand for DiPino the way Jane's servants stood behind us like ostriches. I describe the wine, the food, the music. I tell him how half way through dinner, Jane takes off her white gloves, tells the servants to go, and comes around the table, where she starts cutting my steak into bite-size pieces and feeding me. Then I feed her. I comb my hair in the shine of a dinner plate. We write obscene words in the vegetables and drink our wine straight from the bottle.

Two dogs are in the room, one behind Jane's chair, one in the doorway, lying around like sad tongues on the oriental rugs.

Jane snaps off my top shirt button. She's already looped my tie around my forehead. I touch her face, her hair, her neck, and I am hunting her zipper when the dog behind us growls. It sounds far off. Before I can think *Oh shit!*, Jane is on top of the dog, has knocked it on its back, and is squeezing the life out of its balls. There are black hairs curling between her fingers. Her hand is a fist between the dog's stumpy hind legs that are kicking like a baby in a crib, and the other dog is only a tail sneaking out the door. Jane is on top of the dog, her head buried in its neck, and she is gnawing. One of her shoes, a white lace thing with a single strap and a pink-and-black floral design on the toe, has flown across the hardwood floor and landed upright by a vase. The other one tips like a jet from Jane's foot. The dog is whimpering.

Jane gets up, pats out her dress, and says to the dog, "Out." It limps off like it's got a load in its pants. There is fur in Jane's teeth. Her hand stays curled up the way it was when it had the dog's balls in it.

She says to me, "Time for bed?"

I've gotten to my feet.

She's in close, working on my belt, saying, "I'll just go slip into nothing."

She takes off for the bedroom, and me, listening for the dogs, I slide out the front door. I get my car started about the time the porch light flicks on. Jane comes out, a dog on each side of her. "Hey," she says.

I'm backing down her hundred-foot drive.

She says something to the dogs. I ram the iron gate and hit the street. "Hey," she yells. The dogs are charging me.

I shift from reverse to first while the car's rolling, and she says, "I know where you work." She whistles, and the dogs stop cold. At the corner, I brake stupidly, kill the engine. It's bottom-of-the-pit quiet. I've got two hours before work, so I drive out to Lake Mead, swing around to the far side away from the marina. I wade out up to my knees. The water is flat as a stone, and the moon is up and full. It's the color of Jane's pearls. It's the shape of her collar.

I tell DiPino if I'd had me a bow, I'd have shot the sucker down. I'd have nailed the moon dead center, bulls-eye. I had that much fear and bad temper in me.

I'm winding down, coming to the end of my story, and Ward DiPino is leaning over the counter, one elbow up on it. I was talking and talking, and while I was he stuck one of the pins we have on display into his unpierced ear, and blood is oozing out, is bubbling up on his earlobe. The pin's of a pink flamingo. It nicely balances the fish lure in his other ear. DiPino's dollars have fallen. If you were looking in through the big front windows, you'd think we were doing a magic trick. DiPino's mouth is one inch from my cheek, and his right hand has swung around behind him, gone into his pants, come back up, and put a gun to the tip of my nose. He says, "Ain't life a bitch." The gun is black with a genuine wood handle, and his bloody hand is blue and green and red and not in control of the trigger, the hammer, anything.

He says, "It's a good story. Now let me tell you what it means." He scratches his cheek with the gun, then rests it again on the end of my nose. He says, "What it means is life can get ugly real fast."

"Real fast," I say.

He says, "How much do we have in the till?"

He knows the sign says there is nothing over twenty after dark.

He also knows that isn't true.

I find a couple of hundred, and I return his silver dollars like it's my idea. He puts the money in the Boy Scout leader's hat.

He opens and closes his bloody hand and tells me how he swung by the emergency room, and they said it would be seven hundred and fifty dollars for x-rays, maybe two thousand to fix him up. He got in real tight on the doctor, real close, closer than he is to me, close like they had come to center ring to hear the fight rules, and DiPino held his bloody fist so it touched the doctor's chin. He opened it and closed it, opened and closed it, smiling the whole time. Then he crossed his arms across his chest and said, "Doctor, I'm cured."

He steps away from the counter. Says, "I've got to get myself to a place where I can think. Where I can sit on my butt. You know what I mean?" The gun squats between us. DiPino turns it sideways, sights crazy-eyed down it, then lays it inside his hat with the money. He is standing by the door where the heights are marked so we can tell the cops how tall the thieves are who rob us. DiPino is about six-one. His cigarette tips left. He holds his bloody hand high up and flat out maybe half a foot above his head and says, "I always wanted to be six-six." He cracks the door open, and I can hear his Cadillac out there. It's been running all this time. He says, "I'm not what I used to be."

And his eyes shut down.

He says, "I got to think."

I go to the window and see him yank a U in the parking lot. He points his gun straight up at the moon and fires it once. It's the sound of a champagne cork.

Next to the 7-Eleven is a Hertz car lot. In the last slot, next to the street, is Jane's black Suburban. Her license plate says YBDULL. A car coming up the street lights up the inside of the Suburban from behind, and I see four pointed ears and Jane's head.

I could slip out the backdoor, pull apart the chain link fence where the kids have cut it open, and, if DiPino hits the light wrong, if he has to stop at the corner, I could catch him. I'd bust open his window with my fist, match him crushed-and-bloody hand to crushed-and-bloody hand, and say, "You owe me a ride, at least, blood brother."

I won't do that. Everyone needs their time alone.

I dial nine one one, but I'm not sure what it is I'm going to report. DiPino roars left on Charleston, and the headlights come up on Jane's Suburban. She's let the dogs out. They're backlit, roaming in front of the Suburban, angry. They have their story to tell, their revenge to take. "All men," they will tell me, "will die like the moon." I'll treat them with respect and offer them food and drink. "Sit up to the table," I'll say, opening the door, "The place is loaded. What's mine is yours."

After all, what's at stake here is rebirth.